Crème Brûlée

Ramona Sen is working for *t2*, *The Telegraph*, in Kolkata, where she regularly writes about food, books and fitness, for she is largely preoccupied with food, books and fitness, in that order. She grew up within the venerable walls of Loreto House, where she learnt reading and writing, but couldn't quite wrap her head around '[a]rithmetic'. Nothing, in her opinion, can trump a Wodehouse or a well-baked chocolate pie. This is her first novel, and she'll reply to mails on ramonasen15@gmail.com, when she's not eating on the job.

Urvashi Suraiya lives in Mumbai. Her alma maters are Loreto House and St Xavier's College, Kolkata. In spite of having a dry Bachelor's degree in Commerce, Urvashi is currently honing her skills in graphic design and branding. To know more, visit her website www.designwalrus.com.

Crème Brûlée

a novel

Ramona Sen

Illustrated by Urvashi Suraiya

RUPA

Published by
Rupa Publications India Pvt. Ltd 2016
7/16, Ansari Road, Daryaganj
New Delhi 110002

Sales Centres:
Allahabad Bengaluru Chennai
Hyderabad Jaipur Kathmandu
Kolkata Mumbai

Text copyright © Ramona Sen 2016
Illustrations copyright © Urvashi Suraiya 2016

ISBN: 978-81-291-3977-1

First impression 2016

10 9 8 7 6 5 4 3 2 1

The moral right of the author has been asserted.

This edition is for sale in the Indian Subcontinent only.

To Baba, for providing all the fodder.
Here's hoping you're less disoriented in a place where
no one can steal your chocolates.

Romance should never begin with sentiment.
It should begin with hors d'oeuvres and end with dessert.

—Not quite Oscar Wilde

Chapter One

While humming a tuneless rendition of 'The Blue Danube' into the bathroom mirror, Aabir Mookerjee paused in relief to inspect his full head of hair. Although it had been a year at least since he had had to shave his head, being bald had disoriented him. Silly custom, he thought, as he resumed shaving his chin, having to sport a shaved head simply because one's father had kicked the bucket. As though the late Mr Aritra Mookerjee's soul would attain salvation if his son went around baring his skull to the world. Not that a number of his acquaintances hadn't attempted to look like Vin Diesel or some such bald, muscular hero, but they were fools the lot of them.

Aabir mopped his face with a towel and surveyed the shirts that Mukul had laid out for him. He frowned at a blue-and-brown plaid print. Muttering about his mother's extraordinarily bad taste in men's attire, he tossed it back on the bed. The German Shepherd sprawling on the floor, leapt up at once.

'Bilious, isn't it, Churchill?' asked Aabir, fondly, and the dog immediately rolled over, on what was to become Mukul's new shirt, in drooling assent. Antics like this were the reason why Aabir's mother had objected to dogs around the house, but had, to her chagrin, been overruled by her son and children. There was no stopping the influx of canines around her, mostly large, all slobbery and with a propensity to damage her best shoes. After her husband's demise, she'd had several hysterical breakdowns to drive home the point that any more dogs were unacceptable and Aabir had regretfully returned Churchill's offspring—the pick of the litter, a frisky little thing who had been brought home for only a day and had relieved himself on Mrs Mookerjee's new woven jute carpet from Shantiniketan and nibbled at the elaborate woodwork on her antique dressing table. Later, a distressed Aabir had had words with Churchill, accusing him of irresponsible parenting, but the German Shepherd had seemed not in the least perturbed at having lost the company of his son.

There was a discreet knock on the door. That would be Mukul, sent up to tell him that breakfast was served. *Every morning*. If Aabir had been a less peaceable man, he would have had a thing or two to say to his mother about the daily interruption of his morning toilette.

'I'll be down in ten minutes,' he told a grinning Mukul, upon opening the door.

'The Holy One is here. And oh…Boudi says the *loochi-aloor dom* is getting cold.'

Aabir groaned. The insufferable family purohitmoshai had a nasty habit of turning up uninvited during mealtimes. Absolute pest. Even Aabir's late grandmother had always insisted that the man was an unspeakable sycophant, who had managed to ingratiate his way into the family by filling Aabir's mother's ears with 'all sorts of bootlicking'. The household, with the exception of Mrs Mookerjee, had all sorts of ironic nicknames for this aggravating man who seemed to be a permanent fixture in the house; the servants snidely referred to him as 'The Holy One', for no one was more irreverent than this man of God.

'I don't want loochi-aloor dom,' said Aabir, almost fiercely. He had never been overly fond of the fluffy, grease-filled balls of flour that Bengalis so love to begin their day with. It had been the standard menu for Saturday brunch while his father had been alive, served alongside an equally unhealthy preparation of mutton, in lieu of the lighter potato curry that Mrs Mookerjee seemed to prefer these days. It was little wonder that a heart attack had killed Aritra Mookerjee instantly. Aabir, on the other hand, greatly disliked having to start his day with anything other than a sunny-side-up, cooked only to the point where the yolk was still runny, sprinkled with oregano instead of salt. Mukul looked suitably regretful at the alteration to Aabir's breakfast. Then his face brightened.

'I heard Purohitmoshai say something about a nice girl, Aabirda,' he piped up, cheerfully.

Aabir scowled. 'What has that got to do with me?'

Mukul averted his eyes and grinned. Aabir fought the urge to smack his cheeky head. 'Take away the tea tray when you're on your way out and tell Azim that I like sugar only in the ginger tea. *Not* the lemon tea,' he said, curtly.

Mukul nodded in assent, struggling to retrieve the checked shirt out from under Churchill's sprawling weight. He would be only too happy to point out to the rather pompous chef that he had got Aabirda's tea wrong…*yet* again. Not that Azim was not a fastidious cook. He simply could not bring himself to remember which tea required sugar and which did not. Everyone in the house had their own particular preferences, which varied according to the time of the day, and poor Azim found it all very exasperating. Even Churchill liked to lap up some sugary tea at around five in the evening, while the haughty Lady Mountbatten turned her nose up at anything that wasn't infused with jasmine.

'That shirt is for you,' said Aabir, parting his hair carefully down the left side of his head—he had never parted it any other way. Mukul startled Aabir by bursting into a grin. 'Ought to curb his jubilance, this fellow,' he thought, straightening his collar. 'Too early in the morning to be greeted by yellow teeth.'

He felt mean-spirited immediately afterwards and patted Mukul on the shoulder. 'It will look better on you than it will on me.'

'But Boudi only just bought it for you and she won't like you to give it away.'

'You leave my mother to me and wear that shirt when you see your girlfriend next.'

Mukul's face fell. 'We broke up.'

Aabir tried to look suitably concerned but continued with his careful scrutiny of the tie rack. This was no time to listen to the woes of his manservant. Mukul, however, armed with a new shirt, felt encouraged.

'She eloped with a man from her village.'

'Eloped, did she?' said Aabir, contemplating his choices. *The cerulean tie with the ivory stripes or the cobalt tie with the vanilla stripes?*

'He has more money. He has bought his own flat.'

'Has he?' *Definitely cobalt.*

'But he's much older than I am,' continued Mukul, defensively. 'I will also own a flat when I am his age.'

'Of course you will.' *Good God! What was that preposterous orange affair hanging behind the crested maroon tie?*

'Aatreyeedi put it there,' explained Mukul as his incredulous employer pulled out a sunflower-orange tie from the closet.

'Orange!' spluttered Aabir. 'With purple polka dots! Is she cuckoo?'

Mukul chuckled. It was the popular belief amongst the staff that Aabir's sister did indeed possess an erratic mind.

'Well you do only have blue and red ties, Aabirda.'

'They're not red. They're *maroon.*'

'May-roon,' repeated Mukul, dutifully.

'Loony,' whispered Aabir, quite disoriented. 'Here,' he said, handing Mukul the objectionable article of clothing, 'this is for you.'

Mukul looked as though the Pujas had arrived early. Aabir averted his gaze from yet another toothy grin.

'And by all means, allow Aatreyeedi to see you wearing that.'

'She won't care who's wearing it,' said Mukul, holding up his new polka-dotted tie against his new checked shirt. Aabir blanched.

'Good God! Surely you won't be pairing the two?'

'Why not? It looks colourful. Some of us like colour, Aabirda.'

Aabir ignored the snide barb against his monochromatic wardrobe. He wasn't about to take fashion advice from Mukul.

5

Mukul, who paired checked shirts with polka-dotted ties. Aabir flinched.

'Well I'd be grateful to not be around when you're being colourful.'

Mukul chortled. 'You're funny, Aabirda.'

'I'm glad I can amuse you,' said Aabir, waving at the tea tray, indicating that he had had enough of his manservant.

Mukul didn't mind being waved away. His life had improved greatly since he had been promoted from odd-job boy to manservant on Aabir's return from England. Besides, Aabir, for all his idiosyncrasies, was a benevolent employer. He was neither a tyrant, like his late grandmother, nor a nag, like his mother. Certainly, he was inclined to be wrathful when his shirts weren't arranged in ascending order, depending on the width of the stripes, but all in all, he was a good man. Mukul skipped out with the tea tray and his new clothes, throwing Aabir a parting grin. Aabir hurriedly shut the door.

Oh dear! There was an interfering guest to face at the breakfast table. He decided that he would firmly inform The Holy One that he would not be meeting any *nice* girls and then attempt to get through his unnecessarily heavy breakfast by averting his attention from his mother's disapproving gaze.

⌒

Aabir entered the dining room to find that Purohitmoshai had already launched on dessert. His stomach churned at the sight of the obese *gur rasgollas* floating in a tureen of, what he knew to be, sickeningly sweet syrup. Still, Aabir did prefer the gur rasgollas to the usual white ones and contemplated having one.

'Aabir! Here you are at last! Dressing up in your room I heard?'

'I was *dressing*, yes,' said Aabir, stiffly, 'an activity that some of us can dispense with, it seems.' If religious men in this country must be frequently bare bodied, they should, at least, attempt to be less podgy.

'Aabir!' frowned his mother. Purohitmoshai burped in amusement and patted his capacious stomach.

'That was a wonderful breakfast, Mrs Mookerjee. I've outdone myself.'

'How pleasant,' said Aabir, pulling out a chair for himself at the table.

'Aabir!'

'Good morning, Ma. I'd like some lemon tea to begin with, please. Sugarlessly, this time.'

'Didn't Azim send up your morning tea?'

'With sugar, yes.'

'He never *listens*!'

'I'll have a word with him, Ma. You don't have to kick up another storm about this,' said Aabir, hastily, wishing he hadn't brought it up. His mother's daily outbursts at the servants greatly disoriented him.

'I don't storm,' replied his mother, offended. 'We have loochi-aloor dom as a special treat today. I thought you'd like a change from your usual egg.'

'Thank you, Ma, but I rather like my usual egg. It is, after all, my usual egg.'

The portly purohit chortled.

'I always knew you would grow up to be an odd young man,' he said, wiping his mouth with the pristine white napkin that Aabir had insisted they use. His mother had warned him that white linen was inadvisable in India and Aabir, looking at the large yellow stains on the napkin, realized with a shudder that she had been right.

'Purohitmoshai has been waiting a long time for you this morning, Aabir,' said Mrs Mookerjee. Aabir didn't miss the accusation in her voice. He ignored it and took a sip of the steaming lemon tea that Azim had sent out through one of the maids. It seemed to Aabir that there were more staff than family members in the house and everyday he found an anxious new face hovering around breakfast. This was because, Mukul told him, they were either terrorized by Mrs Mookerjee or terrified by Thakuma on the coconut tree. Often it was both. Aabir, who had been his Thakuma's favourite grandchild, had been intrigued by rumours amongst the servants that the spirit of his late grandmother resided on the coconut tree in the backyard. He had visited the terrace one afternoon, hoping to catch a glimpse of the flowing white saree that Mukul had insisted he'd seen, but nothing other than a couple of shrivelled coconuts had swayed ominously at him. He had retired to his room, disappointed. Evidently, Thakuma only showed herself to the servants of Mookerjee House, terrorizing them in her afterlife as well.

'Aabir,' said Purohitmoshai, burping.

Aabir, about to acquaint himself with the new maid who was setting down a replenished bowl of spicy potato before him, politely turned his attention to The Holy One.

'You have not introduced us to your girlfriend.'

Aabir tried to remember if he had ever really liked this man of God. He certainly disliked him now. 'When the time is right, when the time is right,' he replied dismissively, tearing a loochi into two and wrapping one half around a small portion of potato.

Mrs Mookerjee narrowed her eyes. 'I must meet her before you decide to marry her,' she said.

Aabir looked annoyed, disoriented that he was not being allowed to enjoy the unnecessarily heavy breakfast being foisted upon him.

'There are no wedding bells in the near future, Ma,' he said, evenly.

'Our greatest well-wisher here knows of women who would be happy to set off the wedding bells for you,' said Mrs Mookerjee, glad that she had found an opening. Aabir choked.

'And most suitable women too,' piped up the purohit. 'See, I have pictures.'

From the recesses of his dhoti he pulled out an iPhone and swiped the screen to unlock it. Aabir gaped. Evidently, renunciation had taken on a whole new meaning these days. The purohit saw the astonishment and smiled, albeit a little bashfully.

'A Puja gift from the Mullicks. A very dear family, you see. I've known them for years. In fact, I found the eldest Mullick daughter a fortuitous match. She is now living in Wales with her husband.'

'Of course,' said Aabir, politely. 'To live in Wales is what everyone aspires for.'

The Holy One nodded vigorously. 'That's right, that's right. Her baby will be born in two months.'

Aabir tried to look suitably impressed. 'Well congratulations.

The iPhone must come in useful in your profession.'

'It does, it does. I have all my shlokas saved here. You see, I am getting old and in case I leave a prayer book behind, I have...what is it you say...a back-up?' Clearly The Holy One had missed the sarcasm, but Mrs Mookerjee frowned at her son.

'Back-up,' confirmed Aabir, refusing to meet his mother's eye and pecking away at the loochi-aloor dom instead. Purohitmoshai edged the shiny new iPhone across the table.

'I'm not sure these pictures interest me, thank you,' said Aabir, a trifle coldly. He wished he could raise an icy brow like his sister, a talent that she had inherited from her grandmother. How Aatreyee had managed to fend off his mother, he didn't know. He would seek her advice if she deigned to extend her conversation, with anyone, beyond monosyllables. Perhaps he could scribble down his concerns and have Mukul deliver the note.

'We are trying to show you something, Aabir,' said Mrs Mookerjee, the displeasure now evident in her voice.

Aabir had no intention of being shown anything by this crafty man, especially when he was already feeling the first pangs of having overdone it at the breakfast table. He was beginning to be resentful of this ambush.

'This isn't quite in my area of interest,' said Aabir, to no one in particular.

'Beautiful women are of interest to every man,' chortled the Hole One. 'Unless, of course, they are interested in beautiful men.'

Aabir did not acknowledge the joke. Mrs Mookerjee smiled politely. Purohitmoshai stopped chortling. 'Sreemoyee

Ganguly,' he said, hastily.

'And who, pray, is that?' asked Aabir, politely. The iPhone had slid across the table and had finally come to a halt beside his plate. He caught a glimpse of a bindi that was too large and earrings that were too gold.

'I have had the privilege of tasting mutton chops made by her own hand,' said the gluttonous purohit, smacking his lips to demonstrate his verdict on the aforementioned mutton chops.

'I like mutton chops,' said Mrs Mookerjee, happily.

'I like fish chops better,' replied Aabir. 'Fish takes well to having a crumb-fried surface. This is why fish and chips, as we know it, works so well.'

Purohitmoshai frowned. 'You have become very English in your tastes, Aabir. Not good. Even this restaurant that you have opened on Park Street...only English food?'

'English fish and chips is quite different, I assure you. And I don't hear my customers complaining about my fare,' said Aabir.

'But you are Bengali, Aabir. You must marry a homely girl who will be able to make you good wholesome Bengali food.'

'I doubt there's anything wholesome about mutton chops.'

The purohit looked unsure of what to say next. Mrs Mookerjee looked unhappy with her son's obstinacy.

'Where's Aatreyee? Why isn't she here?'

'In the garden,' was Mrs Mookerjee's non-committal reply.

'What's she doing there?' asked Aabir. 'Isn't it too hot to be out in the garden?'

'I didn't ask,' said his mother, tautly.

'So I'm the only one who gets the third-degree around

here, eh?' said Aabir, cheerfully, getting up from the table. 'Good to see you, Purohitmoshai. Do drop in again.'

Purohitmoshai looked a little taken aback at the abrupt leave-taking and joined his palms, as civility dictated, in uncertain acquiescence. Mrs Mookerjee sighed when her son left the room. 'I must have been bad in my previous life to have been blessed with such difficult children,' she said, tearfully. The purohit patted her shoulder sympathetically.

'I will do everything in my power to help you, Mrs Mookerjee.'

'And you know you will be handsomely rewarded, Purohitmoshai,' sniffed Mrs Mookerjee.

The gleam in The Holy One's eyes was unmistakable.

⌒

Aabir found his sister reclining in the hammock, in the garden, reading *William—the Bad*, while Lady Mountbatten rolled on her back trying to itch a particular spot. She didn't get up to greet Aabir; she was a temperamental Dalmatian attached only to Aatreyee, who she'd taken to like a dog to a couch as a puppy. Mrs Mookerjee had once had nightmares about the house being overrun by Dalmatian puppies; she remembered the movie *101 Dalmatians* only too well. Contrary to her expectations, Lady Mountbatten had fallen asleep in her daughter's arms and other than the occasional penchant for scrabbling at new books from the library, she had displayed exemplary obedience, albeit only to her young mistress.

'Heavyweight reading, eh?' grinned Aabir.

'Yes,' said Aatreyee, without looking up.

'Did you meet The Holy One?'

'Unfortunately.'

'He's fatter than ever.'

'Of course.'

'Did you see his iPhone?'

A pause. Then—'No.'

'He has one.'

'Does he?'

'He had pictures of possible brides to show me.'

'Did he?'

'Did he try to show you pictures of possible grooms?' Aabir chuckled at the idea.

Aatreyee put her book down for a moment and regarded her brother unblinkingly for a moment before resuming her perusal of the antics of William and the Outlaws. Aabir stopped chuckling. How disorienting his sister was.

He cleared his throat. 'I wanted to ask you about the tie you put in my cupboard.'

'Yes?'

'It's orange.'

'Yes.'

'I've given it to Mukul.'

'Good.'

Aabir looked at Lady M, who had stopped rolling on the grass.

'Did you think I'd like the tie?' he asked the Dalmatian, who thumped her tail on the ground and then turned her back to him. Aabir glared at her. Women! Who could begin to understand them?

'Well toodle-oo. I'm off to earn my bread and butter.'

He turned away and started off towards the house. Aatreyee turned another page and stretched out her hand to Lady M, who immediately positioned herself under her mistress' doting fingers.

Chapter Two

Thakuma, seated on the throne of her coconut tree, had a bird's-eye view of the house. She knew, for instance, that Bahadur, the chauffeur, had parked the Contessa in the cobbled driveway in a manner that he hoped would conceal the faint dent on the fender of the car. The fool! As though Aabir would not notice, immediately, the veriest scratch on his most prized possession. This exaggerated fondness for motor vehicles was a trait her grandson had inherited from her husband, and even now, he spent a fortune maintaining his grandfather's 1935 Daimler, so he could be a part of the annual Vintage Car Rally. Thakuma sat up very straight on a leaf. She was looking forward to that Bahadur getting a dressing-down; he deserved it, for all the petrol he stole.

Thakuma was firmly of the opinion that since 'servants are not what they used to be', nearly all of them were dishonest. Hence, Mukul's father, an old-timer who had passed away even before Thakuma's demise, had been questioned about missing tie-pins; Mukul himself was charged of pilfering the mithai specially brought for Aabir from Narayan's Sweet Shop; and Chhaya the temporary maid had been caught, on more than one occasion, plucking precious neem leaves from the tree. Thakuma, mistrustful even in her afterlife, was always on guard, poised to swoop out from the coconut tree at the slightest hint of misconduct from the staff. She often derived morbid pleasure from seeing Mrs Mookerjee tear apart a young and tearful maid for having forgotten to dust the mirror attached to her dressing table. Today, Thakuma spotted her daughter-in-law throwing a slipper at the new odd-job boy who had managed to crease a freshly laundered saree. Thakuma chuckled and hoped the other slipper would follow. Servants these days required thorough training. All these modern-day notions of equal opportunity or some such nonsense needed to be driven out of their minds. Thakuma stopped chuckling only when she spotted Aabir striding towards his car.

Aabir frowned. There was a definite dent in the gleaming fender of his maroon Contessa. He tried to recall if he had had any recent mishaps on the chaotic Calcutta roads, but drew a blank. He was a painfully cautious driver—a quality that made him the butt of many jokes amongst his friends—for he loved his cars dearly; almost as much as he loved the Mookerjee dogs. It greatly upset him to see any of them damaged or ailing in any way.

'Bahadur!' he barked. Aabir rarely barked. But when he did, the servants quailed. Few things are more alarming than a placid man in a temper. Bahadur, napping in the shade of the neem tree in the backyard, sat up with a jolt.

'What have you done?' chortled the gardener. 'Been driving Babu's car again, have you?'

Bahadur scowled at him and buttoned up his white jacket, stained green with the grass. He made his way to the garages where Aabir was standing, looking impatient.

'Well you certainly took your time,' he snapped.

Bahadur looked unhappy. Aabir was in one of his rare foul moods.

'Explain that,' said Aabir, pointing imperiously to the barely visible dent on the fender.

'What, Babu?'

'Imbecile!' roared Aabir. 'Can you not see the fender almost broken into two?'

Bahadur gulped. It was common knowledge that Aabir jealously guarded his cars. Especially the ones he drove himself.

'It...it must have been the motorcycle yesterday...'

Aabir had turned decidedly red, either due to mounting rage or the sun beating down on his face. Bahadur couldn't quite tell which, so he broke off and shuffled his feet instead.

'And why were you out with the Contessa?'

'Boudi...'

As if on cue, a window on the first floor flew open and Mrs Mookerjee's head popped out, her bun curiously lopsided.

'For God's sake Aabir, you're ruining my television serial. First, this good-for-nothing boy, and then you! Nothing has happened to your car.'

Aabir, always respectful of his mother, bit back a scathing retort.

'There is a conspicuous dent,' he said, evenly, 'which I have not caused. And may I advise you to not fling slippers at the help? It is frowned upon these days.'

Thakuma scowled. Her grandson was far more liberal than she'd like him to be. He had no idea at all how to demand service from an underling. This is exactly why she had wanted her son to educate his children at home by a governess, just as she and her brothers had been, and none of them had emerged any worse for it.

'Oh stop exaggerating. There's barely a scratch.'

Aabir breathed hard. Everyday his mother insisted that her headaches were a result of a brain tumour and not because she watched too many Bengali soaps during the day, and it was he who was now exaggerating.

'I bought you an Altis. The Altis is for Bahadur to drive. You know how careless these people are nowadays. I don't like him driving my car. See, he's damaged it.'

'I see. Only when the car is broken, you get upset. My head, it explodes everyday, but you won't take me to the doctor. When I die, you'll regret taking better care of the car than of me,' flung back his mother.

With a huff, Mrs Mookerjee's head disappeared and the window slammed shut. Bahadur was politely inspecting the money plant growing along the side of the driveway.

Aabir got into the Contessa and slammed the door shut. As he started the engine, his mother's voice floated down again. 'At least if you got married, your wife could take care of me!'

Muttering under his breath, Aabir backed out of the driveway with unusual haste. Bahadur made his way back to the backyard to resume his nap.

It was in the afternoons, when the curtains of the Mookerjee House were drawn and shutters closed to enable a deep siesta, that Thakuma was most bored. Even the servants retired after their post-lunch game of cards, after Mukul had forfeited a hard-earned fifty rupees to the clever Azim. The concept of forty-winks did not exist amongst the undead and Thakuma often wished that her spirit had chosen to follow her husband's into that mysterious realm that she knew so little about, instead of latching on to the coconut tree. Not that she didn't love the tree; she had had it planted the year she fled to this house from her father's in Chittagong. Thakuma, particularly pensive during deserted afternoons, would look fondly at the house in which she had spent her most tyrannical years, nurturing the garden, intimidating servants and training Churchill's allegedly blue-blood ancestors. And to think that when she had first arrived, she and Rathindra had tip-toed around the house, trying to keep out of the way of her brothers' wrath!

Thakuma spent much of her time atop the coconut tree reminiscing, as old people are apt to do. Even though she had lived for a century, she had never been lonely and rarely been ailing. A particularly windy day had resulted in a coconut breaking loose from the tree and sailing towards Thakuma, who happened to have been occupying an unfortunate spot under the tree. The coconut had struck her rather hard on the back of her head. And, no sooner had her body hit the soft mud of the backyard, than her soul sailed upwards and made itself at home amidst the very missiles that had resulted in her immediate death.

The panic stricken cries of Mukul had aroused the entire house from its afternoon slumber, and it was then that Thakuma realized the coconut tree was a conveniently strategic location. From here she could see the odd-job boy pull the blanket above his head to drown out Mukul's cries (damn the fellow's cheek; she would pay him a midnight visit), she could see Aatreyee scramble out of a painstakingly-held yogic posture in her room and her dim-witted daughter-in-law hurriedly throw on a dressing gown and pad down the stairs in anxiety. Her beloved dogs had, of course, gathered around her lifeless body and bayed at the setting sun. Thakuma had not been the recipient of such attention since she had fled to Calcutta with a husband, five years her junior. She chuckled to herself as her foolish son's wife sank to her knees in fright and Mukul's horrified cries turned into alarmed gibbering. Only Aatreyee, after overcoming her initial shock, managed to shake Mukul to his senses, summon Azim from the kitchen and have them carry the body back inside.

Aabir's father, Aritra, she noticed grimly, was unnaturally controlled about his grief. Ungrateful wretch, thought Thakuma to herself, waving away a crow attempting to alight on a coconut leaf. After all I've done for him. I suppose he'll just use this as an excuse to build up a fine tab at the Tollygunge Club bar. Rathindra really had spoiled him. She should have put her foot down when he had wordlessly paid every whopping bill that their son had run up at the clubs. Tusharbala's biggest failure had been her son; if anyone had been able to remain unaffected by her iron-rule, it had been Aritra, and no amount of tyranny had beaten any responsibility into him. Needless to say, Thakuma had had little patience for her son and no maternal ties were enough to overcome the aggravation he caused her.

For all her Naziesque bearing, Thakuma had never been

able to withstand the charms of a particular member of the rival family in Chittagong. Towards the latter half of the nineteenth century, the Choudhurys and the Mookerjees had occupied the two largest plots of land in Chittagong, East Bengal. Everyone had got along amiably until Thakuma turned three. It was then that visitors began to remark that little Tusharbala Choudhury was sure to grow into a raving beauty. Rudrangshu Mookerjee had desired his eldest son to be betrothed to the beautiful Tusharbala, but Taraknath Choudhury would have none of it; he had plans for his little Tusharbala; she could marry Governor General's son if she so desired. A deeply offended Rudra Mookerjee forbade his sons from fraternizing with *that* upstart, and the children from both families suddenly found themselves bereft of their playmates. It was no wonder that the scandal spread far and wide, when the headstrong Tusharbala, after having rejected many an impressive suitor, eloped with Rudra Mookerjee's youngest son, Rathindra. While the two fled to Calcutta, Tusharbala's father swore to have his revenge—his eldest son was the district magistrate and if he couldn't have the Mookerjees robbed of land, he could, at least, make their cook disappear. The Mookerjees would drop like rotten fruit when deprived of their daily diet of unparalleled *posto-bora*. It had all happened another lifetime ago, mused Thakuma, seated on the coconut tree, as white as snow.

The marble slab on the pillar outside read 'Mookerjee House', but the sprawling bungalow had really once belonged to a Choudhury. Tusharbala, quaking with fear but plucky as always, had crept into her brother's house in Calcutta, her young husband in tow. A speechless Tirthankar had let his sister in and had reluctantly agreed to keep their whereabouts a secret; Tirthankar Choudhury was no stranger to the obstacles of forbidden love. Years later, although Rathindra had been swiftly disowned by a furious Rudra Mookerjee, Tusharbala was pardoned simply because she was the only daughter of a man who had never wanted sons and had sired three until his fourth and youngest child had turned out to be a beautiful girl. While that kind of unabashed sexism may have incurred public censure these days, as almost everything does, his sons nonchalantly allowed their sister to return to her position as the apple of their father's eye, and a status quo was assumed again.

Thakuma noticed, with the perception granted to her from her place on top of the coconut tree, that Aatreyee had inherited many of her qualities. And a good thing too. It would have been unfortunate if her grandchildren had turned out to be like her incompetent son and his foolish wife, who thought about little else other than a bride for her son. Thakuma noticed with pleasure that Aatreyee had firmly declined to have anything to do with men that either her mother or the sycophantic Purohitmoshai tried to bring to her notice. She wished her grandson would take a leaf out of his sister's book and be less polite. That feather-brained Debjani, aka Mrs Mookerjee, wouldn't be able to recognize a bride suitable for a Mookerjee even if she sailed into the kitchen and cooked up a storm of posto-bora. All the Mookerjees seemed to have a wild appetite for ground poppy seeds fried into chops, even though Aabir liked to claim these days that his favourite snack was a hot, buttered 'croissant a la kiev'—a name he had invented for a croissant that oozed butter like the famed chicken a la kiev. Poppycock. Thakuma regretted her grandson being out of the country at the time of the fatal coconut incident. She would have liked to have left behind a platter of posto-bora for him.

In her lifetime, Thakuma had been a fine cook and had never failed to remind her daughter-in-law that the latter had once brought her an over-boiled egg. Aabir's mother had never, to say the least, thought fondly of his grandmother, even though she had shed copious tears during the memorial service—something Thakuma noted with disgust from atop the coconut tree. Thakuma was not an exponent of the heart-on-sleeve practise and objected to a display of excessive emotion.

The fact was, Thakuma's posto-bora had been unparalleled because of one secret ingredient—a secret that she had refused to let Azim in on, much to his indignance. Azim, who had been a mere boy when he'd arrived at Mookerjee House, considered himself an exceptional chef and would express outrage every time Thakuma locked him out of the kitchen while she whipped up posto-bora behind closed doors. His favourite ploy was to threaten to leave the Mookerjees and offer his services to the Bajorias, who lived next door. Aabir's mother would hurriedly give him a raise; she did not want to lose the invaluable Azim to the nouveau-riche Marwaris, who occupied the sprawling old bungalow next to theirs, only because they had bought it for a princely sum from that destitute, Rajdeep Saha, who had drunk away his entire inheritance. The Bajorias often hosted loud parties that went on into the wee hours of the morning and Mrs Mookerjee was damned if she was going to have her Azim entertain that crowd with his unparalleled hors d'oeuvres.

Thakuma, naturally, did not share her daughter-in-law's

23

admiration for the temperamental Azim. She had, after all, learnt from a far superior culinary force. In Chittagong, her father's chef, Suleman, who had taught her to toss an omelette at the age of six and snuck her fried fish when her mother wouldn't allow her more than two pieces, boasted of an ancestor who had worked in the royal kitchens of Nawab Siraj-ud-Daula himself.

No wonder then that she considered Azim's lightly saffroned biriyani and kababs fried in olive oil for God's sake, hogwash. It annoyed her to have to dress for dinners such as these and yet she diligently pinned her brooch to her saree and exchanged her regular pearls for her dinner pearls, because all her life her mother had insisted that dinner was an occurrence to be treated with respect because it brought the family together at the end of a long day. It was a tradition that her son had destroyed by appearing for dinner in his pajamas and allowing his children to do the same, though she noticed now, that Aabir was not a chip of the old block and was in fact turning out to be a chip of a far older and more dependable block—his grandfather. Every Sunday she watched Aabir wash the vintage Daimler himself, lovingly cleaning the pale leather with special polish. He was even beginning to look like dear old Rathindra, thought Thakuma fondly. The distinguished brow, the broad shoulders, the angular frame. There was an antiquated air about him that was endearing. Thakuma hoped her grandson would have the sense to fall in love with a nice girl and not one of those horrifying modern young things one had the misfortune of meeting these days, who liked fast cars and faster boys.

Chapter Three

Aabir, in fact, had inadvertently found himself in the company of exactly one such modern young thing. When he rolled up outside E&B, he was pleased to find that there was a queue outside the door, despite it being well past the peak lunch hour. He also noted, with pleasure, that not more than a handful were twiddling their thumbs outside Mocambo. The sight of this distracted him into a good mood and he forgot to tick off the cab driver for clearly having tampered with the meter. He had watched its leaping fare with great displeasure, en route from the Calcutta Club, which was not more than forty rupees away from Park Street, and here he was paying almost double. Aabir looked up at the brick red façade of E&B and thought of his favourite review in *The Telegraph* supplement—'The maître d' mops his brow. Petulant teenagers, impatient businessmen, mothers out on a girls'-lunch-out surround him, clamouring for tables at the city's newest fine-dining Continental restaurant. Mocambo is losing some of its business to E&B, less popularly known as "Eggs and Bacon".'

Mocambo was indeed losing some of its business. It was

unheard of for any other restaurant on Park Street, except occasionally Peter Cat—but Aabir discounted that since they were owned by the same gentleman—to boast of a longer queue on a weekend than Mocambo. There was a spring to Aabir's step as he walked in; he had been warned that in Calcutta, people were loath to relinquish the old for the new.

'Aabir!'

Aabir turned around rather startled by the pitch of the voice. There was a petite figure in a rather bilious shade of green waving at him furiously. She looked fairly familiar and he walked towards her table, smiling politely. Now, what is it that she wanted?

'Good afternoon, my dear. What a pleasure to run into you.'

The figure in bilious green grinned up at him.

'This is a really cool place. Sooper cool actually.'

Aabir wasn't sure that he wanted E&B to be referred to as *cool*. Or *sooper* for that matter. Might attract the wrong sort of people; people looking for chicken hot-dogs instead of chicken a la kiev.

'Well, I'm glad you think the food is up to the mark, Miss Basu,' he said, unable to remember her name.

Miss Basu's grin widened. 'You're funny.'

'Delighted to amuse you,' replied Aabir, wondering when it would be a good time to move away.

He noticed that she had just finished tucking into the restaurant's signature dish. 'Excellent bacon,' she told him, wiping her mouth. 'I'm just waiting for my chocolate mousse to arrive.'

'I'm sure it won't disappoint you,' said Aabir, confidently. If there was one thing that he was sure of, it was the quality of E&B's chocolate mousse. It was a special recipe that a dear French friend of his, whom he had met in his Oxford days, had lent him. He had claimed that his grandmother had left the recipe to her family but had taken all culinary skills with her to the grave. The mousse had taken the gourmet world in Calcutta by storm, and in Calcutta, gourmet plays a very important role indeed. Clerks may not religiously fill in ledgers, but they will religiously take frequent tea-breaks, managers are delighted to host interviews at the popular restaurant down the street, news of a fresh eatery will spread like wildfire. Every review, even that particularly nasty one that had criticized E&B for sporting Victorian furnishing, had raved about the chocolate mousse. An acquaintance, who had claimed to frequent Benjarong, a Thai restaurant in South Calcutta, merely for its chocolate mousse, had also changed loyalties.

'I want to entertain some friends here tomorrow, so I'm sampling the place today.'

'In that case, I hope I've given you enough reason to return.'

'Oh yes. Everyone will be knocked out.'

'Excellent, excellent. Just what I want—incapacitated teenagers strewn around my restaurant.'

Miss Basu burst into laughter. 'You're funny. How have you been keeping these days?'

Small talk. Aabir fidgeted with his tie.

'Quite well, thank you.'

He disliked small talk. It made the back of his neck itch rather uncomfortably. Where did he know this tiresome young woman from?

'Well, tell Aatreyee I'll be dropping in on her one of these days. '

'I certainly will.'

Of course. Aatreyee! She did seem to be acquainted with an endless list of odd people. Just the other day Aabir had spotted a person in the sitting room—a visitor for Aatreyee, the odd-job boy had claimed—and he had been unable to distinguish if it was a boy or a girl perusing the book shelf. Androgynous people disoriented him; he didn't understand this blending of the sexes.

A waiter materialized at his elbow.

'Can I get you something, sir?'

'Oh no. Thank you. I've just had lunch. I was on my way to check on the kitchen.'

'Everything's all right in the kitchen, sir.'

'Yeah, stop stressing and have a mousse with me.'

Aabir looked disoriented. He disliked hobnobbing with strange young women, especially at his workplace. He couldn't have his staff thinking that he had anything but distantly cordial relations with any of his guests. People needed little reason to talk and Aabir preferred to steer clear of any sort of 'talk'.

The waiter was already pulling out a chair for him. He found himself sitting down.

'A chocolate mousse for you, sir?'

'A glass of Campari please.'

'Camapari, sir?' Aabir had not been known to order his usual Campari with any meal except dinner.

'Yes. Campari.' Sometimes a man needed Campari even in the middle of the afternoon. Especially when thrust into a spontaneous tête-à-tête with disorienting young women.

'My grandfather used to drink Campari,' said Miss Basu.

'A man of good taste, your grandfather.'

Laughter from Miss Basu. She was continually amused, it seemed. 'That's not what I meant.'

Aabir wasn't quite sure what she meant. This was not what he had planned for the afternoon. How tedious of her, unnecessarily prolonging her meal while there were hungry clients waiting outside impatiently. Everyone was always impatient here, he thought. It was the weather. A man was bound to get fretful when he ruined his collars every day by incessantly trickling sweat into it.

'I hope your chocolate mousse is good. Mousse is difficult to get just right, isn't it?'

Aabir drew himself up to his full height. If there was anything he was offended by, it was insinuations against E&B's chocolate mousse.

'I'll have you know, Miss Basu...' he began, but once again was cheerfully steamrolled.

'There's this neat little tea room opening, you know. Called "The Mad Hatter" or something,' said Miss Basu. 'My cousin is friends with the owner's friend.'

Aabir blinked.

'And I've been given to believe that the dessert selection is fantastic. So you better watch it, mister!' Miss Basu shook her fork at Aabir, who stared at her, stupefied.

'The Mad Hatter? What the devil kind of a name is that?'

Miss Basu wasn't listening. Her dessert had arrived.

'Oh dear Lord!'

'What?' asked Aabir, hurriedly putting down his Campari.

'Oh dear Lord, this is better than I imagined.'

'Well, that's a relief then.'

'You must have some.'

'Oh no. I've had lunch.'

'Don't be absurd. That has nothing to do with anything.'

'I'm quite full.'

'That's no reason to not have a bite of this.'

'Well you see…'

'Oh don't be a bore.'

Aabir's head was beginning to swim.

'No really, I've sampled this mousse many times.'

'Well, sample some more.'

'I assure you, I…' Aabir found a spoon thrust into his mouth. He was unable to gape, but had there not been a deliciously smooth dark-chocolate mousse with a hint of rum filling his mouth, gape he would have.

'Isn't that delicious?'

Aabir nodded.

'I told you. You really should let up a little, Aabir. You're mostly so cute when you're not being stuffy.'

Aabir reached for the Campari and finished it, too dumbfounded to speak.

'My, you're a fast drinker!'

'Uh…'

'I'm going to take my time over this mousse, if you don't mind.'

'Er…'

A waiter murmured something in Aabir's ear.

'Oh dear. It seems there's an emergency in the kitchen.' Aabir was surprised that he was able to invent a glib lie in the midst of such disconcertion.

'Well, I won't keep you.'

'By all means, let me stand this lunch for you.'

'That's sweet,' grinned Miss Basu. She blew him a kiss. 'You're a doll.'

Aabir was not sure that he liked being referred to as a doll. He noticed the waiter grinning and was annoyed. Most people these days knew nothing about discretion. Neither, apparently, did they know anything about subdued attire, he thought, catching a glimpse of Miss Basu's nails, alternately painted pink and violet. Aabir headed towards the kitchen, suppressing a shudder. Perhaps he should consider putting up a notice about acceptable dress codes on the E&B window.

∽

In the evening, Aabir walked back from E&B to the Calcutta Club, where he had parked his car. He settled down into his usual couch in the club library with a sigh of relief; this was the best part of his day. No biliously dressed young women to interrupt his evening newspaper before he went for his evening swim in the tranquil waters of the club pool. The Calcutta Club was famous for its preference for the elderly Bengali, the kind who reserved their exuberance for the Dining Room, especially the weekend buffet.

Aabir looked around the library and felt a warm sense of belonging. He and Aatreyee had spent many hours of their childhood lurking among the bookshelves when they were too young to be allowed into the reading room. Doting bearers had seen that they received more than their share of children's classics. He couldn't quite remember how it had started, but they would hide books that they knew the other was looking for and wait for it to be discovered. Aabir remembered fondly, the thrill of stumbling across a much sought-after book stuffed in the wrong shelf. The old bearer in the library had let the two to play their games. He knew, of course, which book was being concealed on what shelf and often dropped broad hints to the seeker.

It struck Aabir that he had been meaning to refurbish the library in Mookerjee House. His father had left it in sad neglect, being far more interested in the Tollygunge Club golf course and bar than in the upkeep of a spectacular library fostered by his grandfather and Thakuma's brothers. The books, for instance, had been placed in any haphazard order and Aabir was sure that some of the rare Billy Bunter books, procured painstakingly during multiple trips to London in the course of his childhood, had been pilfered. Aabir tried not to think badly of his late father, but sometimes he couldn't suppress the mild annoyance that crept up. For instance, it was just like the old man to overindulge himself on the suckling pig on New Year's Eve and begin the year by incurring a fatal heart attack. His poor mother had been quite prostrate with grief.

A headline in the city supplement caught his eye—'The Mad Hatter in Calcutta'. He frowned; he had forgotten about The Mad Hatter during his day's work. He read on to discover that a tea room was about to open near Elgin Road, and all sorts of delicious tidbits were on the menu. 'The crème brûlée is an item to keep an eye out for, or a tongue, as the case may be,' said the review.

Aabir glared at the printed page. He did enjoy a well-made crème brûlée; it was one of the few non-chocolate desserts that he was fond of. But this Mad Hatter business seemed like bad news for the likes of E&B. His chocolate mousse, for example, was in jeopardy.

'Aabir Mookerjee, isn't it?'

Aabir looked up to find a rather arresting woman standing before him. It wasn't that she was beautiful, but the length of her skirt, the height of her heels and the arch of her brows would certainly make heads turn.

'I'm afraid you have the advantage, madam,' he said, getting to his feet.

'Meenakshi Chatterjee. I've heard so much about you.'

'Oh, have you, now? What an alarming thought.' Aabir tried valiantly to not notice that her bosom was difficult to miss.

Miss Chatterjee laughed. 'A sense of humour is always so attractive in a man.'

Aabir shuffled his feet, clutching at the newspaper. 'If you insist, if you insist.' He did so hate these chance encounters. Women threw him quite off his guard.

'If you're the same Aabir Mookerjee who's opened that all-night joint on Park Street, I have to say that that is an excellent place.'

'I'm glad you approve, Miss Chatterjee.'

'No really. We desperately need a nice place to stuff our faces in after the night clubs close and what's better than some bacon to soak up the alcohol, I say!'

'I…yes if you say so,' said Aabir, imagining E&B swarming with drunk teenagers at an unearthly hour of the night. This was not why he had insisted that E&B be open all night.

'Wasn't that your idea?'

'Well, I took a late flight into the city one night, and there simply was no good food to be found. I'm not sure I enjoy stalking in and out of the cold, marble-floored hotel lobbies. I quite detest them actually.'

'Oh? Most people love hotels.'

'Yes. Well.' Aabir paused, abruptly. 'I decided E&B would be open all night to serve their signature dish—eggs and bacon.'

'Only eggs and bacon?'

'Only eggs and bacon,' repeated Aabir, firmly.

Meenakshi pursed her lips. 'I like eggs and bacon.'

'Who doesn't?' asked Aabir, horrified.

'Er...vegetarians?'

'Oh. Them.'

Meenakshi laughed. 'You're funny, Aabir. May I call you Aabir? Will I be seeing you in the Crystal Room today?'

'Crystal room? What crystal room? Why in the crystal room?'

'The banquet hall. It's called the Crystal Room!' Meenakshi looked surprised that Aabir seemed to be so ill-informed about the nomenclature of the club's various rooms.

'Oh, that crystal room. I see. No. I don't usually kick up my heels in there.'

'It's Mr Datta's silver anniversary today. He's invited a crowd.'

'I'm happy to announce that I'm most certainly *not* one of the crowd, Miss Chatterjee.'

'Oh call me Meenakshi. And that's absurd. I'm quite sure an invitation had been sent to you.'

'Well, I don't know the man from Adam.'

Meenakshi frowned. 'I'll admit I'm disappointed. I was rather looking forward to getting better acquainted with you.'

Aabir shuffled his feet. 'Oh…er…'

'I'll see you around anyhow then,' said Meenakshi. She squinted and leaned forward suddenly, reaching for the paper in Aabir's hand. He leapt back, taken by surprise at her unexpected lunge. 'The owner of this new restaurant…' began Meenakshi.

'Owner? Restaurant?' stammered Aabir, feeling the heat rising to his face.

'This Mad Hatter joint that's opening. She's launching her cookbook at the Tollygunge Club next weekend.'

'Oh. That. I think it's a tea room. Not quite a restaurant. Let's not confuse it with restaurants, eh?'

Meenakshi shrugged. 'Tea room then.'

'Writing a cookbook is she?'

'Launching it at Tolly Club. I'll have a look at the bulletin board for you, if you'd like.'

'Oh no, thanks. I'll take a look when I'm in Tolly next.'

Miss Chatterjee smiled. 'I'll see you around there perhaps,' she said and swung around, departing as suddenly as she had appeared.

Aabir sank into his favourite armchair, quite bewildered.

The bearer in charge of the library sought Aabir out. Aabir rather liked the chap; always smiling and willing to run an errand or two for a pack of cigarettes.

'Everything well, Sabir?'

'Oh yes, Mookerjee saab. Will you be issuing a book today?'

'Oh no, thank you.'

Sabir hesitated. 'I thought I should inform you, saab, that the pool is quite crowded this evening.'

Aabir looked annoyed. 'Is it now?'

'Yes. You see, a lot of members are in the club today, what with Mr Datta's party and the special Afghani buffet.'

'So, Mr Datta's having quite a party, eh?'

'Oh yes. He celebrates his anniversary in the club every year. People are saying that when he becomes president, he will mark the date in the club calendar as an official event.'

Aabir, mostly unaware of the who's who of the club, looked only mildly interested.

'I don't think he can do that.'

Sabir laughed. 'Of course not, Mookerjee saab. People just like to say these things.'

'When is Mr Datta going to become president?'

'Who knows, who knows,' said Sabir, secretively. 'There is a recipe to becoming the president. I am sure that when you are old enough, you will become president too.'

Aabir looked amused. 'Heavens, no. I don't think I want to.'

Sabir looked astonished.

'Not want to be president, saab! Why! Some people plan their lives around becoming president of this club!'

Aabir looked amused. 'Such exaggeration, Sabir.'

'Truth, saab. That was Nandan Chatterjee's daughter you were talking to, saab.'

'Nandan Chatterjee, the current president?'

Sabir nodded vigorously. 'C134.' The club staff had a remarkable memory for membership numbers. 'He has a beautiful daughter.'

'Er…yes…if you say so. Why is this of interest to me, Sabir?'

Sabir shuffled his feet. 'Just saying, saab.'

Aabir was rather fond of the man. Sabir's father had

been library bearer when Aabir had been a mere boy, and had often given him and his sister a chocolate on Sunday evening, while they waited for their father to come and take stock of the books that they wanted to borrow for the week. But sometimes Sabir tended to be nonsensical.

'Don't *just say* silly things, Sabir.'

'Yes, Mookerjee saab. You must think about becoming president, Mookerjee saab. You would be good for the club. And everyone likes you.'

Aabir sighed. 'And how would you know this?'

Sabir nodded knowingly. 'Bearers hear things, saab. People don't notice us and so we hear everything.'

Aabir felt uncomfortable and a little bit feudal. Then Sabir left the reading room and he sank further into his couch. He would have to forgo his swim this evening. He was glad he hadn't known of Mr Datta's party. He disliked large parties; they tended to be so *loud*. It occurred to him that the Calcutta Club did not boast of a stern dress code for women and was momentarily surprised by it since the men were expected to be immaculately turned out. He turned his attentions back to the newspaper, quite forgetting about bare bosoms in the face of the endangered chocolate mousse.

Chapter Four

It was a sultry morning. Aabir—who had been woken up far too early by an enthusiastic Churchill drooling into his ear, a long leash hanging from his mouth—was in his study, relaxing his overworked muscles to the crescendos and decrescendos of Mozart's Sinfonia Concertante. He had turned up the volume very high, so as to drown out his mother's irate voice from the kitchen, as she demanded to know why Azim had added fried eggplant to the neem leaves when she had specifically asked him not to.

Aabir disliked these daily shenanigans with the servants; they disoriented him. This is why he liked to leave the house in the morning and return only after his mother was quite done with her vociferous disapproval of the servants' conduct. He had known of course, when he'd returned from England, that living in his ancestral home again was going to need some adjusting to. He remembered how surprised his friends had been to hear that he was going back to live with his mother. But in Calcutta, all sorts of eyebrows would have been raised if he'd simply shifted out of home to his own place when their rambling old house clearly had more than enough rooms. Not that he didn't love the old house. And he was glad that he had had the foresight to have the old gramophone restored. Calmed his nerves, they did. The speakers lining his study wall did not do justice to the trill on the E-string. He had had them installed in a rare moment of brashness, influenced by raving reviews from his friends, who, he later discovered, listened to shockingly ghastly music. Deaf Leopard, he believed, was the name of one such band. The horror.

Occasionally, Aabir would emerge from his room and find his study occupied by his sister and her yoga mat. Upon objection, she would pause the horrifying music that she liked to listen at a deafening volume and look at him coldly. He would have to retreat of course, which he thought was very unfair, since it was, after all, *his* study. Aatreyee had inherited all of Thakuma's fierceness, but unlike Thakuma, did not hesitate to turn the ferocity on him. At least Thakuma had allowed him all sorts of freedom, including allowing him to dip her round, thin arrowroot Marie biscuits into her afternoon tea—a thing he had done well into his teens.

Aabir missed Thakuma. She had been an admirable woman, eloping with his grandfather in an era when such social crimes were unforgivable. He had fond memories of her sneaking out posto-bora for him from the kitchen, when his mother had forbidden him to eat any more. Thakuma, who would tear Mukul to shreds if she was able to spot a single crease on her saree, had also nursed their three-month-old Pug all night through a horrific and fatal illness and single-handedly dug a grave for the puppy in the wee hours of dawn because she refused to relinquish the corpse for the corporation to dispose of. This had left an indelible

39

impression on young Aabir, more so than the sight of his dog-fearing mother shedding tears at the untimely death of a helpless little thing.

A crash behind him made Aabir look around with a start. Of course it was Mukul upturning the Russian literature set placed precariously on a low bookshelf, between elephant-shaped book-ends. Mukul habitually upturned that set. He was incapable of walking into the study without sending the Russian books to the floor, book-ends and all. Aabir sighed. Mukul grinned apologetically.

'You've put them back upside down, Mukul,' said Aabir, patiently, turning Mozart down to a gentle murmur in the background.

Mukul dutifully turned the set the right way up. 'This shelf is too close to the door,' he said, by way of explanation.

'Of course it is. And that is why we all upend those books on our way in.'

Mukul looked confused. 'Do you also?'

Aabir sighed. Sarcasm was continually lost on his manservant. 'Try to remember that the books exist, Mukul,' he continued, still patient.

Mukul nodded. 'Boudi wants you downstairs.'

Aabir grimaced. It was only eleven in the morning. His mother would not have been done with giving Azim his daily dressing-down and Azim would still be in the midst of dark threats about leaving to offer his services next door. Aabir was not sure that he wanted to be caught in this cross-fire.

'What for?' he asked Mukul, who shook his head.

'I don't know, but she did say that it was important that you go downstairs quickly.'

Aabir sighed. His languorous morning was ruined. He was certain that he was going to be sent on some nasty errand. He couldn't understand why Aatreyee was never sent to take old Mrs Ghatak across the road freshly cooked pomfret or give the neighbourhood milkman a piece of her mind for mixing water into the milk. If anybody was suited to go around imparting a piece of her mind, it was Aatreyee. Aabir disliked having to give anyone a piece of his mind unless it was imperative, or for that matter, having to take freshly cooked pomfret for Mrs Ghatak and then being rewarded with a comprehensive list of her ailments.

What it was that Aatreyee occupied herself with, remained a mystery to all the members of the Mookerjee House. It was true that she had shot off to the London School of Economics, but had thereafter returned home and spent her days closeted behind the doors of her room. Any curiosity was immediately quelled. Even the relentlessly curious Mrs Mookerjee had been unable to get to the bottom of her daughter's activities, possibly because Aatreyee displayed such little activity. Aabir liked to think that his sister was secretly working for the Indian Intelligence. Only that would explain her tight-lipped mystery. Of course, with her icy exterior and striking beauty, Aatreyee would be the ultimate double-agent in an international espionage. Perhaps, like Mr and Mrs Smith, she too led a double life; scholar in the Mookerjee library by day and machete-wielding Catwoman by night. Like James Bond, perhaps she too had lovers in distant countries who she had rescued from the throes of death. Perhaps she had had spies who'd loved her, or a diabolical affair with Dr No and had left behind a trail of blood-stained bullets that had been for his eyes only, from India with love.

Aabir frowned. His thoughts were trailing off into the disturbing. He wished to display no subconscious curiosity of his sister's dangerous liaisons. That was sure to be a Freudian symptom of some sort and Aabir was quite certain that Freudian symptoms were something to be steered clear of. Not that it didn't occasionally amuse him to have his imagination run wild. Once he had talked animatedly about the workings of the secret service, as he understood it from Ian Fleming and Frederick Forsyth, but much to his disappointment, his sister's disinterest betrayed nothing. Of course, it was a studied disinterest that she practised.

Aabir went downstairs and found his mother in the drawing room, fanning herself furiously, in spite of the air-conditioner being on.

'What has been bothering you again, Ma?' asked Aabir.

'That Azim. He *never* listens. He always thinks he knows better. Once again he has omitted to add the fish eggs to the curry.'

Aabir looked sick. He detested fish eggs, especially in curry. Evidently so did Azim, God bless his stubborn soul.

'Dreadful,' he said to his mother.

Mrs Mookerjee stopped fanning herself and looked up at her son. 'What are you doing for lunch tomorrow?' she asked.

'Why? Nothing in particular. Look in at E&B I suppose, since it's the weekend. I like to ensure that the restaurant is running seamlessly on a Saturday.'

'I know someone who would love to eat at E&B.'

Aabir frowned. His mother's friends bored him. Oft

repeated tales from his childhood could not keep him diverted for long.

'I don't want to occupy an unnecessary table during a Saturday afternoon,' he said, testily.

'In that case, you'll have to take her out elsewhere.'

'Who?'

'Sudeshna Sengupta.'

'And why is she in need of a meal?'

'A very nice girl from a very good family.'

Aabir breathed hard. 'What does that mean?'

'Now, there is no need to look so annoyed…'

'It seems to me that there is every need to look so annoyed,' fumed Aabir.

'Don't overreact. She is very pretty.'

'Of course she is.'

'And very well-educated. Loreto House—St Stephen's…'

'And from where did you dig her up?'

'Purohitmoshai of course.'

Aabir scowled. That damn purohit.

'He knows of a few well-established families. We cannot have you married to just anyone, can we?'

'I don't recall saying that I *was* going to marry anyone.'

'But it's time to, don't you see? I'm only asking you to meet this girl over lunch…'

'Well, I don't think I'm going to,' said Aabir, stubbornly.

'You have to. She's expecting a call from you.'

'What!' yelped Aabir.

Mrs Mookerjee sighed. 'I spoke to her mother this morning, Purohitmoshai gave me the number. She sounded quite nice.'

'I'm sure she did,' growled Aabir.

'We both agreed that it would be wonderful to have you meet Sudeshna.'

'And what has Sudeshna to say?'

Mrs Mookerjee shrugged. 'I'm sure she's awaiting your call.'

Aabir gnashed his teeth.

'There's really no need to be so ferocious about it,' said Mrs Mookerjee.

'Really, Ma. Sometimes you cross all limits,' snapped Aabir and stormed out of the room. He met his sister on the landing of the stairs.

'Ma has forced a date on me,' he complained.

'Oh?'

'There is a girl awaiting my call.'

'Ah.'

'It's absurd!'

'Hmmm.'

Aabir looked at his sister exasperatedly. His exasperation turned to curiosity when he noticed what her arms were piled with. 'What are you doing with those ragged old cushions?' he asked.

Aatreyee fixed a stern gaze on her brother.

'I thought you'd thrown that green one away months ago,' persisted Aabir.

Lady Mountbatten growled and Aatreyee continued down the stairs. Aabir watched her descent thoughtfully. For a moment he imagined that the portrait of Thakuma on the wall winked at him. He stared at it for a while and then sighed. Entertaining strange young women for lunch was not his idea of an ideal Saturday.

⁓

Aabir had changed his shirt thrice. He hadn't been able to decide between the starched white shirt, the white shirt with the hairline-navy stripes or the white shirt with the violet-dress stripes. He settled for the navy stripes and a crested tie that he thought would complement his new grey coat, recently tailored by his father's old faithful, who had had the same clientele for the last decade or so. Aabir admired the perfect half-an-inch of cuff emerging from the coat sleeves and decided that Mr Lahiri had indeed not lost his touch.

He wondered about the young woman that he was about to meet. Her voice over the phone had not been the high, feminine tone that he had been expecting. In fact, as he had stumbled around niceties, his neck itching furiously under his collar, she had succinctly brought the conversation around to the statistics. Did he want to meet her in the Tollygunge Club for lunch? The question had befuddled him for a minute. On one hand, he didn't want the bearers to talk about the strange sight of member M141 with a woman. On the other hand, he would at least be on familiar turf as opposed to the disorienting gleam of a five-star hotel.

'Or Zara always has some interesting cocktails and Spanish appetizers, if you're up for that,' the non-high voice had continued.

'Tollygunge Club works for me,' Aabir had said immediately. He had once had the unfortunate experience of being invited to dinner to the aforementioned Zara. The music had disoriented him. Young girls in adult clothing had disturbed him. And when he had asked for coffee, he had been told that only alcoholic Irish coffee was available. These were not, of course, concerns that had bothered any of the others in the party, who had enjoyed both their spiked coffees and the appalling background music. Aabir had made his early excuses and escaped to the Tollygunge Club to avail of the fried fish and chips. The 'Shamiana' could always be depended upon to dish out excellent fried fish and chips. Yes, Aabir decided, this infernal meeting must certainly happen on home ground.

Now, as he rolled into the parking lot of the said home ground, he felt his collar slowly dampening; it was inadvisable to don coats at just any time of the year in Calcutta. Aabir was also beginning to feel distinctly uncharitable towards his mother. Adjusting his silver bull-terrier cuff-links, he strolled towards the Shamiana, which Sudeshna had chosen over the Belvedere Room. She liked to look out into the rolling golf fields from this casual diner and Aabir had silently agreed. One of the reasons why the Shamiana—which derived its name from the large cloth canopies erected during out-door activities, even though it was more like a concrete hut—was so popular was the magnificent view it offered of the club's vast golf course. The Shamiana was a pleasure to sit in during any season, which was a lot to say about any eatery that was not air-conditioned in a city that sweltered eleven months out of twelve.

When Aabir entered, the Shamiana was brimming over with late-Saturday brunchers, some nursing cold beers after languorous golfing. He headed towards a corner-table, nodding at members he was on nodding terms with. He hadn't spent more than an uneasy five minutes, fidgeting with his cuff-links and tapping his shoes noisily under the table (a nervous habit that he had developed in school and which had not made him popular in examination halls), when a rather well-dressed figure stopped at the table.

'Aabir?' said the non-high feminine voice.

'You must be Sudeshna,' said Aabir, getting to his feet and immediately stretching out his hand, which he hoped was not clammy.

'You're exactly how I'd imagined you'd be,' she said.

Aabir didn't quite know what to say. Had he imagined Sudeshna at all? Here she was, definitely not slender but in a very flattering burgundy dress. He noticed that her nails were *not* painted in different colours but had elegant white tips. His mother had clearly exaggerated her beauty, but she did have rather large, expressive eyes.

'I'm not quite sure how I imagined you,' he confessed, drawing out a chair for her.

'I don't blame you. I suppose your mother wrangled this as much as mine did.'

'Well…'

Sudeshna swivelled in her chair.

'Mind if I order a fresh-lime?'

'Oh, by all means, go ahead,' said Aabir, embarrassed that he had not immediately offered.

'Boy!' boomed Sudeshna, across the Shamiana.

Aabir winced. He wasn't sure that bearers could be summoned as 'Boy' in this day and age anymore, and he was certain that a nod would have attracted attention eventually, even though the club staff had made a career out of avoiding eye contact with members.

Duly, a bearer strolled up to take an order for a fresh-lime water and Campari with Sprite.

'Campari. Nice,' said Sudeshna.

'Is it?'

'So much better than these nouveau-riche people sitting around on a Saturday afternoon, guzzling beer. It's sad how the nouveau-riche quotient in the club has risen over the past few years.'

Aabir winced again. He hoped that her non-high, booming voice could not be overheard by the aforementioned nouveau riche.

'Ah…yes,' he said.

'And of course the class-four staff has become worse than ever. The other day, one of them actually tried to stop my brother from entering the Belvedere Room in trainers.'

'I believe that a dress-code prevails in the main dining room, yes,' said Aabir.

'So it does, but you know how these low-class people like to throw their weight around when they're in any position of authority.'

Aabir poured himself a stiff Campari. This talk of class-four staff and nouveau riche was making him decidedly uncomfortable.

Sudeshna looked around. 'Did you know Mr Yadav is having an affair with Mrs Iyer?'

A mortified Aabir turned red as the teenagers at the next table turned around rather interestedly at this bit of scandal.

'I'm not sure who they are,' he muttered, wondering how he could politely suggest that scandalous tales should not be regaled loudly.

Sudeshna burst into what could only be referred to as booming laughter, and several heads turned, mostly amused, since the Tollygunge Club members were known to be less stuffy than the ones who frequented the Calcutta Club. Aabir was far from amused at having had heads turn at him. He liked to avoid having heads turn at him, especially if they were turning because he was in the company of a loud female.

'Not know Mrs Iyer?! Why, she's the Miss Chatterjee of Tolly, only married.'

'What do you mean?' stammered Aabir, not sure he wanted to hear the answer.

Sudeshna put down her glass of fresh-lime and stared at him.

'My mother told me that you're frequently at Cal Club?'
'I am.'

'Well, surely you must know Nandan Chatterjee's daughter. She's infamous. Throws herself at any half-good-looking man. And everyone knows, of course. We all talk about her.'

Aabir gulped. Had Miss Chatterjee thrown herself at him? Was the Calcutta Club talking about him? Was he then, a half-good-looking man? Aabir had never been able to decide whether he was a good-looking man or not. His oldest friend, Rana Raina, often insisted he was a goblin in fancy clothes, but he suspected that was all a part of his friend's questionable sense of humour.

Aabir loosened his tie, crests be damned.

'Everyone knows?' he croaked, in a strangled voice.

'Of course. She's never been subtle. Be careful or you're next.'

Aabir choked. 'I am?' The words emerged in a definite squeak. Aabir cleared his throat.

'Well you're Cal Club's new eligible bachelor. Naturally, you're talked about. It's not often that the club can boast of young and handsome blood.'

Aabir cleared his throat again; these days women seemed to be determined to embarrass him.

The bearer was making his way towards their table, possibly to take the lunch order. Aabir's gaze shifted to a figure just entering the Shamiana. He decided that that was a lot of leg on display and averted his eyes to the head attached to the legs. His heart stopped as he recognized Miss Chatterjee's perfectly aquiline profile.

'I'm dreadfully sorry,' he told an astonished Sudeshna, getting to his feet. 'I've just remembered a vital engagement that I had this afternoon. Do forgive me.'

50

'But...' stammered Sudeshna.

'I do beg your pardon. I know this is quite unforgivable of me...'

Aabir's voice faded as he backed out of the side entrance. Once he was out, he sprinted towards the parking lot. Aabir rarely sprinted. When driven to sprint, it would not be wrong to assume that he had been thrust into an acutely uncomfortable situation.

Sudeshna Sengupta sipped her fresh-lime and wondered what she could have possibly done wrong. Miss Chatterjee slipped into the green upholstered chair, unaware that she had disrupted what could have been a fateful meal.

Chapter Five

Kimaya Kapoor looked around E&B and decided that she wanted to be seated at one of the centre-tables; now that her book was all set to be out in stores, she didn't need the privacy of the corner tables. Unlike most regulars, Kimaya didn't like the idea of settling on a single corner and making it hers. She skimmed the menu for something she hadn't already tasted and decided that she'd take a stab at the croissant a la kiev. What on earth was that? Intriguing. She looked up to catch the eye of the young waiter who was wont to hover around her, clearly uncomfortable in his coat-tails. Sure enough he was hovering again, his pen quivering anxiously in his hands. Kimaya smiled at him. It was popularly agreed that Kimaya Kapoor's smile was her greatest asset, her strongest weapon. When she smiled, crying babies would begin to gurgle, grumpy old men would beam toothlessly and poetic young men would frantically scribble eulogies. The anxious waiter sighed, forgetting for a moment that his ridiculous uniform was making him the laughing stock of his friends. When he caught the steward's glowering eyes, he backed away, muttering Kimaya's order until he reached the kitchen.

Kimaya flipped through a copy of her brand-new cookbook. Hardbound, illustrated, thirty-five recipes. She had spent eight months in her kitchen with the redoubtable Tanuja, experimenting with their favourite tea-time recipes. She'd had to put it all down quickly to have the book out by the time their tea room opened, and holing up for hours in this quaint little joint on Park Street seemed to be the only way to do it. At home, Pepper the Cocker Spaniel had no concept of personal space and insisted on curling up on the laptop if she decided that all work and no play was making her mistress very dull indeed. Kimaya was going to miss frequenting E&B. Now that The Mad Hatter was all set to be Calcutta's grand tea-time attraction, she was going to have little time to perch herself in this curious little place, sampling the best of the a la carte. The chocolate mousse really was everything it was cracked up to be, and Kimaya didn't even *like* chocolate!

On occasion she'd spotted the proprietor of E&B pottering around. She'd heard him discussing the pros and cons of a dress code with the maître d', but the latter had gently coaxed him out of the idea. When prevailing times did not insist that white-collar workers sport a white collar anymore, it would be fatal for business if wealthy customers were prevented from entering the restaurant simply because they were in flip-flops. The proprietor had grunted, unconvinced, and Kimaya had fought the urge to laugh. She'd taken a peek at him and decided he couldn't be much older than she was, though the fact that he was wearing tartan suspenders was a dead give-away that the man was a relic. Or a dandy. Good-looking though, had been Kimaya's fleeting thought before she'd turned her attention back to the text in bold that emphasized the importance of never overdoing the blowtorch over the crème brûlée—an axiom that the proprietor of E&B would have heartily agreed with.

～⌒∽

Burnt dessert however, was the last thing on the mind of the proprietor of E&B. Aabir Mookerjee disliked drama and he could sense a drama of the Grecian sort brewing in the air—Purohitmoshai seemed to be worked up. Aabir tried to bury himself deep within *Indian Summer*, hoping that The Holy One would not be so rude as to interrupt someone steeped in learned preoccupation.

'I am very disturbed,' announced Purohitmoshai.

Aabir sighed inaudibly behind his book. Of course the man was exactly the sort of person to be so rude as to interrupt learned preoccupation.

'Very disturbed.'

Aabir felt a surge of annoyance at Mukul, who had shown this man into the study instead of the drawing room. What was the point of having a formal drawing room if all sorts of hoi-polloi were going to traipse up the stairs and invade his private space? There was some excuse about the sitting room being occupied by carpenters mending the antique settee near the window, but Aabir was put out nevertheless. The infernal house was always crawling with carpenters or plumbers or electrcians; something or the other was continually on the verge of collapse.

The purohit cleared his voice audibly. Aabir sighed again and put away his book.

'How pleasant to see you again, Purohitmoshai. How are you?'

'I'm very disturbed,' repeated The Holy One, firmly.

'Are you? How distressing.'

The door opened and Mrs Mookerjee hurried in, looking flustered. 'So sorry to have kept you waiting. We nearly caught the jackfruit thief red-handed.'

'Has someone been stealing our jackfruit?' asked Aabir, surprised.

'I've been telling you about it for a *week*, Aabir. You *never* listen. Just like Azim!'

Aabir wondered if he should be insulted at being compared to their cocky and disinterested cook, but decided it was too much trouble and far too hot to move himself to take offence.

'So, who was the thief?'

Mrs Mookerjee looked peeved. 'We didn't catch him.'

'Or her, as the case may be,' said Aabir.

'It's some brat who's been taking advantage of the afternoon siesta.'

In Calcutta, afternoon siestas begin after lunch and extend well into dusk. In the more affluent neighbourhoods, shops firmly and noisily bring down the shutters at one in the afternoon and lazily begin to open after five. This gives jackfruit-thieves plenty of time to indulge in their lawlessness.

'Probably one of the servants who work at the Bajoria's.'

'I would advise you to not voice these unfounded accusations, Ma.'

Mrs Mookerjee sniffed petulantly.

'She's been trying to steal Azim for years!'

'You know, Azim just makes those false claims when he wants a raise, don't you?'

Mrs Mookerjee sniffed again. 'They're not all false.'

The purohit cleared his throat. 'I came to say…' he began, looking offended.

'Yes, do say, Purohitmoshai,' said Mrs Mookerjee, contritely. 'I got carried away.'

Aabir grunted.

'Have you had some tea?'

'No, I don't want any today, thank you.'

'Special tea from Kashmir that a friend of mine brought back for me.'

'Well, if you insist…'

Aabir grunted again.

Mrs Mookerjee pressed a bell and seated herself in the comfortable armchair opposite the family purohit.

'Now, do tell. To what do we owe this pleasant surprise?'

'Well, excuse me. I think I want to read in the garden,' said Aabir, who had a nasty feeling that the purohit's pleasantries would be most unpleasant for him.

'Don't be rude, Aabir.'

The door opened and Aatreyee walked in. 'Saki,' she said, looking directly at Aabir.

'Room,' replied her brother, with a jerk of his head. Every now and then Aabir liked to challenge himself by matching monosyllable for monosyllable.

'Tell Mukul to bring up a cup of the *kehva*, will you?'

'How are you, my dear? So beautiful you're becoming each day. I…' began The Holy One. The door shut firmly after a retreating Aatreyee. Purohitmoshai looked astounded.

Mrs Mookerjee coloured with embarrassment, while Aabir suppressed a snort. He must applaud his sister the next time they accidentally met around the house.

Purohitmoshai's surprise gave way to further outrage. 'My honour has been affronted, Mrs Mookerjee,' he began, pompously.

'Oh dear! You must not mind Aatreyee. She's...'

'Not by your daughter, though God knows her manners could improve...'

It was Mrs Mookerjee's turn to look offended.

'...by your *son*.'

He turned dramatically towards Aabir, who braced himself behind his book. The Grecian drama he had been expecting was beginning to unfold.

'What do you mean?' asked Mrs Mookerjee, astonished. 'Aabir, put down that book!'

Aabir put down that book, even though he resented being addressed as though he were an errant child.

'What has he to say about his meeting with Mrs Sengupta's daughter?'

Mrs Mookerjee turned towards her son. 'Why, I think it went all right. I haven't had any scathing reports and I'd like to count my blessings.'

'The scathing reports have come from the girl, Mrs Mookerjee,' said Purohitmoshai, ominously.

Mrs Mookerjee blanched. 'Whatever do you mean?' She turned to her son, 'Aabir, what does he mean?'

'Yes what do *you* mean?' asked Aabir, trying to muster indignant curiosity.

'You *know* what I mean.'

'No, I most certainly do not,' snapped Aabir, resenting this interference in his affairs.

'You walked away!'

Mrs Mookerjee gasped. 'What does that mean?' she cried.

'He left the girl stranded in the middle of the Tollygunge Club.' The Holy One seemed to be taking unholy joy in causing Mrs Mookerjee discomfort.

'Oh, let's not pretend that that's the same as leaving her stranded in the wilderness.'

'Well, foxes do emerge at night, I've heard.'

'This was during the day when she was in no danger of being mauled by foxes. Besides, I had my reasons for walking out.'

'Walking out?!' wailed Mrs Mookerjee. 'Oh Aabir! How ungentlemanly of you!'

Mukul entered the room with the tea tray and Aabir caught the Russian literature set on its way to the floor.

'Really, Mukul!' he snapped.

'Sorry, Aabirda. Those books are always near my elbow.'

'And yet they miraculously keep out of the way of everyone else's elbows.'

Mukul nodded in vigorous agreement.

'Mukul, that's enough. Learn to be more careful,' said Mrs Mookerjee, anxious to return to the subject of her son's appalling behaviour.

Mukul left the room and Purohitmoshai slurped noisily from the cup. 'My honour has been put at risk,' he said, smacking his lips. 'After all, it was I who had suggested Aabir's name.'

'No, I do understand…' said a distressed Mrs Mookerjee.

'And the Senguptas have a wide social circle. You understand that they might...'

'Might?' prodded Mrs Mookerjee, her eyes like saucepans.

'*Talk*,' said Purohitmoshai, leaning forward, conspiratorially.

Mrs Mookerjee gasped again.

Aabir slammed *Indian Summer* down on the writing table, his rare temper flaring.

'Now that's quite enough, Purohitmoshai!' he snapped.

Mukul and the odd-job boy, who had sensed excitement from the moment the purohit had arrived, had been hovering outside the closed study door, hoping to catch something worth talking about to Azim, who was going to be insufferable now that he had *almost* caught the jackfruit thief. When Aabir raised his voice, they clutched each other in excitement and pressed their ears to the keyhole.

'I will not have you entering our home and distressing my mother.'

'Aabir...' said Mrs Mookerjee, always alarmed when her son flew into a rage.

Purohitmoshai started. He had not expected the peaceable Aabir to work himself into such a heat.

'It is intolerable that you have taken it upon yourself to interfere in my affairs.'

'It is your mother who asked for my aid in the matter of your marriage and I do what I can, as a man of God, to help those who seek my assistance,' said The Holy One, pompously. He proceeded to drain his cup of kehva as though the act of speedily finishing the beverage proved that he was a benevolent man of God.

'Unless I ask you to aid in the matter of my own marriage,

please steer clear of the subject, Purohitmoshai.'

Mukul wriggled outside, wishing Aabirda didn't always insist on speaking in English. Made it very difficult to follow the thread of what sounded like a mighty interesting altercation. The two boys outside the room tried to piece together what was happening from the strains of Bengali from Purohitmoshai and Mrs Mookerjee. The family purohit was popular with no one other than Mrs Mookerjee, who gladly gave in to his sycophancy. In fact, it had been he who had arranged her fortuitous match with Aabir's father and, in a rather devious way, had managed to oust the purohit who had previously been serving at the house. It was a mystery that Thakuma had allowed this substitution to happen and the servants had been instantly wary about this new scheming induction into the household. Mukul's father had warned him to sneak the greedy purohit the occasional fruit from the kitchen so that Mrs Mookerjee would not be induced to fire him. Mukul duly kept an emergency pile of particularly fat bananas under a sack in his room. The purohit, in return, promised to put in a special prayer for him. Mukul decided that he wouldn't be surprised if the fat purohit had managed to wheedle his way into the good books of Maa Durga herself.

'You have hurt me with your lack of gratitude, Aabir,' The Holy One was saying, turning on his air of the long suffering martyr; it was an air that he assumed very often to get his way.

Aabir looked disgusted. Mrs Mookerjee had retreated into petrified silence and Thakuma had descended from the coconut tree to have a better view of the row that was ensuing. She would never forgive herself for having allowed her feather-brained daughter-in-law to replace the good-natured purohit, who had conducted all the religious festivities of the house before the intrusion of this imposter. Now she willed Aabir to throw him out for good from the premises of Mookerjee House.

'I'm afraid there will be no apologies from my end,' said Aabir, firmly. 'I have already extended my apologies to Sudeshna. Your taste in women is, of course, impeccable. Loud-voiced snobbery and vociferous gossiping are exactly the traits I seek in my bride.'

Purohitmoshai gaped. Aabir polished his glasses and settled back into his chair. 'Allow me to resume my reading,' he said, picking up his book.

Mrs Mookerjee and the purohit sat in silence for a minute or two.

'It's sultry today,' said Mrs Mookerjee.

'I suspect it might rain,' replied Purohitmoshai. 'In which case, I must take my leave.'

'Do…do return soon,' faltered Mrs Mookerjee.

Aabir coughed. The Holy One looked aggravated and lumbered to the door. He glared at the giggling servant boys standing a few feet away.

'Haven't you anything to occupy yourself with?' he snapped as he passed them.

They giggled harder. Mukul was even pointedly eating a banana, the cheek of it all. The purohit would have to warn Mrs Mookerjee about that boy when this unpleasant business was over. God knows, that young Aabir seemed to have put on all kinds of airs after he had returned from England. Young people these days just could not be depended upon to remain trusting. Aabir's mother, on the other hand, had been devoted to him since she was ten, when he had allowed her to fill her purse with all sorts of edible offerings from the altar during Saraswati Puja. But both her children seemed to be distinctly unpliable.

Purohitmoshai met Aatreyee on the stairs. 'I'm leaving,' he said, pointedly.

'Good,' said Aatreyee. Lady Mountbatten, who had never liked the smell of the purohit, wrapped her teeth around his dhoti. Purohitmoshai looked alarmed.

'Hey!' he said.

The giggling faces of Mukul and the odd-job boy appeared over the banisters. Aatreyee looked on, a hint of a smile flickering on her lips.

'The dog...' yelped Purohitmoshai, as he tried in vain to detach himself from the jaws of the Dalmatian.

'Lady,' called Aatreyee, languidly.

It wasn't often that Mountbatten ignored the voice of her mistress, but sometimes a foul smelling purohit was far too delicious a treat to forgo.

An agitated Mrs Mookerjee appeared at the stairs. 'What's happening? Get that dog off him!' she cried.

Aatreyee started up the stairs. 'She means no harm,' called Aatreyee, as she made her way up.

'Dalmatian!' cried Mrs Mookerjee. 'Stop it! Shoo!'

Lady Mountbatten tugged harder at the ends of a dhoti that Purohitmoshai was struggling to keep from unravelling. Aatreyee stared incredulously at her mother. 'Really?'

Mrs Mookerjee turned upon her daughter in fury. 'You see? You see why I detest these creatures? Completely unpredictable! Ready to maul a man at no provocation!'

'Everything in this house is out of control!' shrieked Purohitmoshai, hopping on one ankle.

Aatreyee had turned a fine shade of pink, as she often did when she was worked up. In spite of giving the impression of one who had had an artery rupture inside her, she managed a haughty glare at her mother.

'Lady!' she called.

Lady M tore a sizeable chunk of raw silk from the ends of the dhoti and gambolled up the steps. It was the last straw. Purohitmoshai stormed down muttering dark threats. Aabir, who had emerged from his room to see what the squealing was all about, glowered at his mother.

'Of all the ill-informed, preposterous things to say!' he snapped.

'Don't talk to me...' began Mrs Mookerjee, on the launch of a hysterical tirade, but Aabir had spun around and was turning back to his study. He noticed Aatreyee's clothes seemed unusually dirty and wondered about it. He would have mentioned it, but she had already disappeared into her room. Churchill, who had been roused from his afternoon siesta too late, came sniffing up the stairs and stopped at Mrs Mookerjee's feet.

'What?' she spat.

Churchill looked up, the whites of his eyes growing, resentfully.

'Come,' called Aabir at his study door. Churchill bounded forward. 'Don't want her sending you away, now do we?'

Of course if there was any question of Churchill leaving, so would Aabir. Mrs Mookerjee may have forbidden any more dogs, but the ones inhabiting Mookerjee House would not be abandoned and even she would not have the heart to desert them.

Aabir settled into his armchair with a sigh. Women did complicate matters so. Regrettable, that business with Sudeshna. He was not a man who enjoyed being anything but perfectly courteous, but really, the thought of being noticed by that Chatterjee woman in the presence of a gossipy girl…the need to bolt had been too strong. He contemplated sending her an apologetic box of chocolate mousse; surely the city's best chocolate mousse would absolve him of any unpardonable behaviour.

He wondered how he had ever managed to get himself entangled with a woman once. Not that that had turned out well. He turned his attentions back to *Indian Summer*; he preferred to dwell on the indiscretions of Lady Mountbatten—the historical Edwina, not the purohit-hating Dalmatian—than his own.

63

Chapter Six

Rana Raina, stepping out of the Shamiana, found his old friend grimacing at the bulletin board. He crept up behind him and thumped his shoulder. Aabir Mookerjee jumped and swivelled around.

'Sup?' grinned Rana Raina.

'What do you mean *sup*?' asked Aabir, crossly. 'Everyone knows *sup* stands for *supper*.'

'Everyone has evolved since then. You're a few centuries old.'

'Don't be rude. What are you doing here? I thought you were in Amsterdam.'

'Landed last night. So jet-lagged. Also, I was really craving a club sandwich.'

'Club sandwiches are ungainly. Having to chew on three layers of bread makes anyone look clumsy.'

'They're delicious. You're an idiot.'

Aabir Mookerjee glared at his oldest friend, questioning their association as he often did. It was a friendship that had started at the impressionable age of five, over a shared love for cream-filled rum-balls at the Calcutta Club bakery, which

Mr Mookerjee and Mr Raina would often have packed for the other's son. Aabir's father was not known to preserve relationships, but his friendship with Ratan Raina had never run its course, something that had greatly peeved Aabir's mother, who had always judged the man by his corrupt politics.

'Amsterdam was bloody brilliant,' Rana Raina was saying, with a gleam in his eye that told Aabir exactly what it was about the place that had appealed to him.

'There's no end to your debauchery.'

'Prude.'

'Stop wasting my time and tell me if you want to accompany me to this book launch.'

Rana Raina looked suitably horrified. 'Why the hell would I want to do that? Who attends book launches?'

'People who *read*?'

Rana Raina ignored Aabir's scathing tone and peered at the bulletin being pointed out to him. 'The Mad Hatter's Tea Party is a book launch?' he asked.

'Evidently.'

'...invites you to the launch of Kimaya Kapoor's cookbook, *The Mad Hatter's Tea Party*, as a prelude to the opening of her tea room on Sarat Bose Road...' read Rana Raina. 'Hey! This sounds pretty cool. Also, Kimaya Kapoor eh? Sounds like a babe. Let's go.'

Aabir looked disapproving. 'Attempt to not be a perpetual boor, will you?'

'Me? Bore? I'm never a bore. People hang on my words like Ethan Hunt was hanging off the Grand Canyon.'

'Boor!' hooted Aabir, at the end of his tether. 'The graceless animal. You ignoramus...' with a frustrated snort he stalked away from his friend towards the book launch in the garden.

'You don't know who Ethan Hunt is, do you?' cried Rana Raina gleefully, trotting after Aabir.

'I suspect the knowledge will not move my universe. And you're not suitably dressed at all for a book launch.'

'Nobody dresses for a damn book launch,' said Rana Raina, stubbornly shoving his hands into the pockets of his Bermuda shorts.

The two stood at the periphery, surveying the crowd. A tea-table was laid out at the side and another table stacked with cookbooks stood beside it.

'Where's the writer?' asked Rana Raina.

'I don't know the writer. But oh dear, I do know this woman. Quick. Let's get some tea.'

The gaping Rana Raina caught Aabir's hand to impede his progress to the tea-table and Meenakshi Chatterjee came bearing down upon them, smiling beatifically.

'Oh, so you did come to the launch after all?' she said. 'I'm so glad.'

'This is my friend Rana Raina,' said Aabir, wondering if Meenakshi Chatterjee possessed any article of clothing that was not tailored to display ample amounts of leg or bosom.

'Rana Rana? What a funny name!' laughed Miss Chatterjee.

'Rana *Raina*,' corrected Rana. 'My father had an odd sense of humour and I think he would have been pleased if I'd been called Rana Rana.'

'Have you ever thought of changing your name?'

Aabir thought she was being rather rude, seeing that she had just met the man, but Rana Raina was not offended.

'Of course not. If it weren't for the name, good-looking

ladies like you wouldn't notice me, would they?'

Disgusted, Aabir made his way towards the tea-table, leaving Miss Chatterjee to laugh tinklingly at Rana Raina's shameless flattery. Tinkling laughter always set Aabir's teeth on end.

'Sausage rolls. Cucumber sandwiches. Almond cheesecake,' he mumbled, reading out the cards placed before every dish. He stopped before the cheddar scones.

'Not eating?'

Aabir turned around to face a woman who seemed to be wearing a skirt stitched from newspaper. She looked familiar, he thought. He decided he must have seen her milling around the club.

'I'm going to. I never miss an opportunity to partake of good food. Do you know who the writer is?'

'That would be me,' smiled the young woman.

'Oh capital! I was just going to pick up the book. It's only tea-time snacks eh?'

Aabir noticed she was laughing and looked puzzled.

'I'm sorry,' she choked. 'You said *capital*. Old men in books say *capital*!'

Aabir sighed. 'This isn't the first time I've been accused of being an old man in a book. But I assure you I'm a youngish man in the real world.' He stretched out his hand. 'Aabir Mookerjee. I wouldn't half mind being an old man in a book.'

'Kimaya Kapoor. I'd pick up that book.'

'This is quite a spread you've rustled up.'

'Try a cucumber sandwich.'

'I was eyeing the cheesecake. I have such a sweet tooth.'

Kimaya smiled. 'Try both.'

'These are the thinnest sandwiches I've ever had. I must admit that I do love a thin sandwich.'

'Ah. Stuffing your face, I see,' said a voice behind them.

Aabir scowled. 'Miss Kapoor, it's my displeasure to introduce to you Rana Raina,' he said, without turning around.

Rana Raina grinned. 'I'm his oldest friend because nobody else would have him.'

'Put a lid on your impertinence and try some of this cake. It's very good.'

'I'm going to pick up the cookbook,' said Meenakshi Chatterjee, sounding a little peeved.

Aabir turned around. 'Meenakshi Chatterjee,' he said, by way of introduction.

'Oh, I know Mia,' said Kimaya. 'We used to be in school together.'

'Oh?' Aabir was surprised. *Mia* certainly hadn't mentioned it.

'Yes. Kimaya used to be such a mouse of a girl.' That laugh again.

Aabir coughed. 'Oh? Honing her culinary talents, was she?'

'Quite right,' smiled Kimaya. 'I hope you're all going to pick up a book.'

'Most certainly,' said Aabir.

'Don't let him,' squealed Meenakshi, putting an arm out to hold Aabir back, who was immediately discomfited by the pressure of her palm on his shoulder. 'He owns a restaurant. He'll just steal your ideas.'

Kimaya's face lit up. 'Oh, of course! I've seen you in E&B! It's one of my favourite places.'

'Flattered,' said Aabir, wondering if it would be rude to

shrug off Meenakshi Chatterjee's hand. *Women*. Kimaya's eyes rested momentarily on the raspberry pink nails on Aabir's shoulder.

'I've been there. The waiters are in coat-tails. I was so amused.'

'Aabir's like that. He's from a different century,' said Rana Raina, his mouth full of a banoffee cupcake.

'I thought the place had a certain ambience,' said Kimaya.

'Thank you,' beamed Aabir.

'The food is just divine,' breathed Meenakshi. 'The chocolate mousse is simply...'

'Oh, I did like the caramel custard better...'

'But...' stuttered Aabir.

'I don't really like chocolate. But for what it's worth, the mousse was an excellent mousse, in spite of it being chocolate.'

Aabir stumbled back, dislodging Meenakshi's hand from his shoulder. 'How does one *not really like* chocolate?' he asked, aghast.

'One likes other flavours. Like caramel. Or red velvet.'

Aabir snorted.

'This is a doomed friendship,' said Rana Raina, solemnly.

'We'll salvage it,' grinned Kimaya.

Meenakshi scowled.

'I'll judge the book by its cover first,' said Aabir, firmly.

'Come on. I'll sign a copy for you.'

She strode to the book counter, her newspaper skirt rustling as she led the way.

'Is that a skirt made from newspaper?' hissed Rana Raina, his mouth full of sausage roll.

'Must you talk as you eat?' hissed Aabir in reply.

'It's a skirt that has a newspaper print, for God's sake,' said Meenakshi. 'Can't you see, it's made of cloth? *Men.*'

'Ohh,' said the men, in simultaneous revelation.

'How odd,' said Aabir.

'Interesting,' said Rana Raina.

'Shall I sign two books?' asked Kimaya, turning at the counter.

'Of course,' said Aabir, elbowing Rana Raina, who he knew was opening his mouth to refuse a book.

'Of course,' repeated Rana Raina, pulling out his wallet and shooting Aabir an injured look. 'And I'd like to give Meenakshi here a copy too.'

Aabir rolled his eyes and Meenakshi beamed at him.

'What a sweetheart.'

'I try. I try,' said Rana Raina, with an exaggerated shrug.

Aabir looked down at the scrawl on the first page of *The Mad Hatter's Tea Party*.

To Aabir, it read, *there's more to a tea party than chocolate.*

'We'll agree to disagree, shall we?' he said, smiling.

'Perhaps later I'll wage war,' grinned Kimaya. 'My restaurant is opening on Friday evening at 4.00 p.m. Drop by. Everything will be on half-price.'

'Excellent strategy,' said Rana Raina.

'I think I will, you know,' said Aabir, flipping through the cookbook. 'Your recipes look sinful.'

'Thanks. I must corner that journalist there and insist he give me a good review.'

'I'm happy to threaten him,' said Rana Raina.

'Er...'

'Don't listen to him,' said Aabir. 'And thank you for a

pleasurable evening indeed.'

'The pleasure was all mine,' laughed Kimaya. It was a captivating laugh. Her mouth was *very* wide. Aabir smiled as he watched her dashing away.

'I'll see you two again, then?' said Meenakshi, a trifle stiffly.

'Of course,' said Rana Raina, eagerly. 'I'm frequently in Tolly you know.'

'So am I. Though Aabir is more the Calcutta Club person, I would think.'

'Aabir is a silly old man.'

Aabir had left the two of them behind and was walking thoughtfully out of the garden. He had had an idea.

Chapter Seven

Azim was in a rare good mood. He had not snapped at the part-time maid this morning for not having taken out the garbage bag in time to the municipal truck that lumbered around at ten every day. Azim insisted that he would not have the day's rubbish piling up in his kitchen and the maid did not hesitate to retort that taking out the garbage was really his job. This was Azim's cue to bristle and the usual battle, along with the all-too-familiar repartee would ensue, until Mrs Mookerjee stormed in and put an end to it. It was a well-rehearsed play which the actors did not seem to tire of.

Today a black-faced Azim had parked himself at the kitchen door as the maid rushed in, three minutes too late. There was nothing that ruined the day for Azim more than having the maid race after the truck as it rolled away. The odd-job boy took his position in the vicinity of the kitchen, waiting for her to return; he hadn't yet tired of the regular kitchen altercations, unlike Mukul or the gardener, who cheerfully continued with their morning chores in spite of the raised voices; they were all too familiar with the script.

Mukul had ruined it that morning by sauntering in and letting Azim know that Ranada and his sister were expected for lunch, and that Aabirda wanted to know if Rana's favourite *chingrimaacher malaikari* could be whipped up on such short notice. Azim, waiting near the kitchen door that led into the garden so that the maid would not be able to evade him, beamed. The odd-job boy was startled. Azim's dark mutterings when the maid had dashed out, three seconds too late, had encouraged him to take a seat in the corner of the kitchen, next to the potato basket, and expectantly await an uproar. The boy looked forward to a well-played scene, especially one that was soundly rehearsed and where the participants had mastered righteous indignation as though the accusations being levied were completely unexpected.

The Mookerjee House afforded many a scene and the odd-job boy thought it well worth his time to stick on, even though his mother insisted that he wasn't being paid enough and Azim was rather a drag to work with. But Mukul had been very nice to him indeed and had often let him share his Saturday-night rum if he agreed to dust Aabirda's study. Once however, he had burnt a garment belonging to Mrs Mookerjee while attending to his chores under the after-effects of country liquor procured by Babloo, the sweet-shop owner's son. The light chiffon material had been hastily thrown away, much to Mukul's displeasure, who liked to throw his weight about when no one was looking. Mrs Mookerjee was convinced that it must have come unclipped from the clothesline and fluttered away and Mukul had darkly warned the odd-job boy that although Boudi would never discover the truth, Thakuma on the tree knew everything that was going on inside the house and she was sure to pay him a visit.

The odd-job boy had cracked up; this business about Thakuma manning the house from the coconut tree never failed to amuse him. Mukul was aggravated by the blatant disrespect for Thakuma's revered ghost. He often insisted that Thakuma liked to breeze by his windows the days he was neglectful of his work. For instance, when he had omitted to confess that the clock in Aabir's study chimed only at night and not during the day because he had been tinkering with it, Thakuma's lorgnette had glimmered at him, threateningly from the backyard. The coconut tree was considered sacred. One no longer lounged in its shade on a hot summer day, and even when coconuts were being plucked, it was done after a solemn prayer to the ghost of Thakuma. Of course it was only the servants who had insisted on these rites since Thakuma's own relatives displayed a shocking irreverence for the subject.

The argument about Thakuma's residence on the coconut tree was also the subject of a well-rehearsed scene. It was most often started by Mukul, who would dutifully announce a sighting of the venerable spirit, followed by a grunt from Aabir and a disbelieving snort from Mrs Mookerjee. Aatreyee remained silent on the subject, never betraying even a sceptical monosyllable. This would be enough for Mukul to wax eloquent on the subject of Thakuma atop the tree.

'She's there, I tell you. I've *seen* her.'

'Of course you have,' said an indulgent Aabir, who had long given up keeping an eye out for his grandmother.

'Her spectacles reflect the sunlight.'

'Oh so *that's* what that odd sunny patch in the dining room is!' exclaimed Mrs Mookerjee.

Mukul debated for a moment if that was sarcasm and decided that it was.

The odd-job boy knew that it was time now for Aabir to send Mukul on a silly errand.

'She watches us all,' said Mukul, ominously.

'Fetch me my matchstick-shaped bookmark, will you Mukul?'

'Where is it?'

'In one of the books in my study.'

The odd-job boy grinned at the familiar sequence that followed—suspicious hesitation from Mukul, raised eyebrow from Aabir, muttering exit by Mukul.

Today, however, the odd-job boy was out of luck; there were no scenes to be had, in the kitchen or out of it. Azim, unmindful of the maid who had been late with the garbage bag, left his post by the kitchen door, beaming.

'Rana? Coming here? It's been so long.'

Mukul nodded. 'Do you remember how he once hid snails in Aabirda's cupboard?'

Azim chuckled. 'Amongst his shirts too. Aabirda was so angry!'

'He even gave Aatreyeedi a joke plate once and when we put food on it, the plate leapt up and spilt gravy on her clothes.'

It was common knowledge that Aatreyee rarely bought new clothes and refused to have even her oldest garment manhandled. The maid had never heard the end of it when Aatreyee had discovered an old yellow shirt drying in the sun, right-side-out. Aatreyee insisted on hanging out her clothes inside-out. Preserved the dye, she declared. The servants disagreed, but silently so. When Rana Raina's practical joke had resulted in an irremovable gravy stain, the blood had drained from Aatreyee's face. Only an irrepressible Rana could have remained buoyant under that glare, although he had appeared the next day armed with a new skirt. A frozen-faced Aatreyee had accepted it and had, of course, given it away at the earliest opportunity. It was rare for Aatreyee to take a liking to any article of clothing chosen for her.

The odd-job boy listened to Mukul and Azim, exchanging anecdotes, puzzled. Clearly this Rana fellow had once been a riotous fixture at Mookerjee House. It was not for everyone that Azim would have whipped up the elaborate chringrimaancher malaikari at such short notice.

⌒⌒

'Time stands still in your house, you know,' said Rana Raina, cracking open a beer bottle and putting his feet up on a footstool. Aabir looked at him sternly.

'Exactly. This is why my favourite couch has remained my favourite couch and I resent other people occupying my favourite couch.'

Rana Raina grinned at him. 'You're a funny guy, Aabir.'

'It was not my intention to amuse you,' said Aabir, settling down in the chair opposite his friend, Campari in hand.

'And yet you continue to amuse me. Listen. I've been meaning to tell you. That woman...' Rana Raina made an offensive gesture to indicate that the woman in question had a well-endowed bosom. Aabir rolled his eyes.

'Which woman are we to objectify yet again?'

'Oh please,' said Rana Raina. 'As if you don't objectify women.'

'Indeed I may have had a shallow moment or two, but I certainly haven't made a shameful career out of it like *some* people I could name.'

'Balls,' said Rana Raina, rudely. 'Anyway. This Meenakshi female. I could totally just...'

Aabir held up his hand. 'Pray, spare me the gruesome details of what you could totally just. I know what you mean when you say you could totally just.'

'I was going to say *totally just take her out to dinner*, you twisted bugger.'

'Don't lie to me Rana Raina. You've never taken a woman out to dinner if you can help it.'

'Of course I have!' cried Rana Raina, indignantly. 'Two and a half times in my life!'

'Half?' asked Aabir, curious.

'I made the dinner reservation. We just never ended up making it to dinner. We got a little carried away...' grinned Rana Raina.

Aabir rolled his eyes. His friend's excesses did not take him by surprise. Rana Raina's misadventures with the opposite sex had begun at a tender age and Aabir had always been the discreet observer. As far as women were concerned, he was inclined to be a tad reticent. Of course there had been that girl with glorious dimples, who had sat in front of him in the orchestra class. If there was anything that had been an impediment to his progress from Second Violin to First Violin, it was the smell of lavender in her hair. Aabir, of course, had never uttered a word to her, except once to lend her an E string when hers had snapped.

'But Meenakshi, you know,' Rana Raina was saying, 'she's

different. She's more than just a sex kitten. I don't know why she has the hots for you. But I can turn that around.'

'What!' exclaimed Aabir.

'She has the hots for you, man. Haven't you felt it? Such an ass!'

'Good God. No, I had not noticed! I just assumed she was the flirtatious sort.'

'She is,' grinned Rana Raina. 'Of course if you're going to be preoccupied with women who bake delicious cookies…'

'Don't be absurd.'

'No judgement there. Way to a man's heart is his stomach. Age-old truth. Socrates said so.'

'Er…he didn't.'

'Fine, fine. But you know what I mean.'

'I do not.'

'Don't be difficult. Attractive woman. Not at all fat… always a good thing. Noticed her collar bones. I like a woman with prominent collar bones, don't you? Long eyelashes… that's supposed to be a thing of beauty.'

Aabir fixed his friend with a glare. 'Noticed all that, did you?'

'Of course. I know what to look out for. Especially when I see my oldest, most idiotic friend grinning like a half-wit…'

'I was not grinning…!'

'Then there's that smile that makes you look twice…maybe because it stretches end to end like a Cheshire cat…'

'No one ever accused Julia Roberts of being a Cheshire cat!' exclaimed Aabir, testily.

Rana Raina grinned. 'Exactly. No reason why you shouldn't try to score. Especially since you've been languishing ever since the English Rose episode.'

Aabir sipped his Campari and said nothing.

'How long has it been since you returned, weeping?'

'One year, two and a half months. And I was *not* weeping.'

Rana Raina whistled. 'Way too much time, man. Dogs have recovered faster from the loss of their masters.'

'That's a horrid metaphor.'

Rana Raina shrugged. 'Anyway. This Kimaya seems a decent catch. Great legs. Did I mention her great legs?'

'If you're quite done…' threatened Aabir.

'All right, all right. I'm just setting you on the path of virtue.'

'I believe you,' retorted Aabir. 'But since you brought her up, I was pondering the possibility of…' started Aabir.

'Possibility of…?' said Rana Raina, eagerly sitting up.

'…of a business association. E&B's chocolate mousse might be outstanding, but the other desserts are just about good.'

'Aha…but she hasn't even opened her restaurant yet.'

'I know. It's just a thought.'

'It's a good thought. Hang on to it. Though The Mad Hatter's tea party isn't really your style, is it?'

'Nothing about her is my style,' said Aabir, vehemently. 'That Mad Hatter business…ridiculous newspaper skirts…her culinary skills are her only saving grace.'

Rana Raina smiled and leaned back in his chair. 'When are we going downstairs for some malaikari?'

◦~◦

The Holy One laboriously dipped a biscuit into the tea that the odd-job boy had set down before him.

'Is Aabir home?' he asked Mrs Mookerjee, who had evidently been aroused from her afternoon siesta.

'No. He stepped out with an old friend who had dropped in for lunch.'

'I see,' said the purohit, his mouth full of sodden biscuit. 'I have found another girl.'

'Another one?' asked Mrs Mookerjee, eagerly.

'Is she pretty?'

'She's charming.'

'But not pretty? Or fair?'

'It's difficult to be objective about these things, Mrs Mookerjee.'

Mrs Mookerjee frowned. 'What does she do?'

'She is pursuing a PhD in English from Jadavpur University.

'Not bad. I don't know how I'm going to get Aabir to see this one. He's being so difficult.'

'Young people these days just don't value family life.' The purohit clucked his tongue in disapproval.

'It wasn't like this in my time. We all wanted to get married and raise children and have a healthy family life.'

'I think it's unfair that your children want to deny you the pleasure of being a grandmother,' said the purohit, pompously. 'Very unfair. Very unfair.'

'I don't think they realize how important it is to me,' said Mrs Mookerjee, a little defensively. 'I'm sure this year hasn't been easy for them either, you know, what with losing their father and everything.'

'It's been more than a year since Aritra died. Aabir should be doing his duty by you.'

Neither of them realized that in the backyard a coconut tree was swaying rather threateningly. If Mukul had taken the trouble to look up, he might have noticed the wrathful glint of Thakuma's lorgnette. Thakuma may have disliked the family purohit, but her patience for her dunderhead daughter-in-law often ran thin.

'Sitting there, wallowing in his sycophancy,' she grumbled. 'He's obviously after something, you fool!'

Thakuma had had little patience for her daughter-in-law since the day the latter had stepped foot into Mookerjee House as Aritra Mookerjee's new bride. Not that it had been easy to survive Thakuma's regime, but young Debjani, lacking in both wit and culinary skills, found herself continually out of favour with the presiding matriarch. The fact that she whimpered every time one of the large family dogs—the Mookerjees did not like small dogs—reared up at her, did not increase her charm. Thakuma refused to call any of her dogs to heel; after all, any dullard knew that a dog leaping up to his human was only a joyous greeting!

Debjani's father-in-law, on the other hand, had been rather kind and brought the new bride gifts every time Thakuma had reduced her to tears. Of course Thakuma claimed that this was a tactic that Debjani employed, merely to extract trinkets from her mild father-in-law, but Rathindra Mookerjee could also be stubborn when he wanted; after all it was not by being a doormat that he had won the stately Tusharbala's affections.

'I do so want a baby to cuddle again,' sighed Debjani Mookerjee, finding in the purohit a willing and sympathetic audience.

'Of course you do. And it is only right that you should

have one. I'm trying my best to find a suitable girl for our Aabir,' said the purohit, picking up his eighth jam-filled vanilla cookie.

'Purohitmoshai,' said Mrs Mookerjee, turning to the purohit as he chomped on his umpteenth chocolate cookie, 'you are my only friend.'

The coconut tree swayed some more.

'I have a special reward for you, you know. If you can find a bride for my Aabir, you will be handsomely rewarded.'

A coconut crashed to the grass as the purohit's eyes gleamed. He smiled beatifically at Mrs Mookerjee. 'That is very kind of you, my dear,' he said. 'But I'm doing this because I'm so fond of you. After all, it was I who fixed you up with Aritra. Else you would have been married to that horrible Shankar Dey, who had kept more parrots than servants in his mansion.'

Debjani Mookerjee shuddered at the thought of being married to Shankar Dey and his parrots. Yes, if it hadn't been for her father's purohit, she would never have met the dashing Aritra Mookerjee in the crowded pandal that Puja, so many moons ago. She sighed unhappily. It's true her husband had been prone to leading an excessive life, but he *had* been so handsome. She was certain that any grandson of hers was going to be just as dashing.

'All the more reason for me to reward you, Purohitmoshai. I am not ungrateful for everything that you have done for me.'

The fat purohit wiped the tea-stains of his mouth and wobbled to his feet.

'I must take your leave now, but call me when we can fix a meeting with Aabir and Pragya. Let it be soon. Her parents are also keen that she be married.'

'Of course, of course. We might have to spring it on him. Why don't you just bring the girl home one day? I'll convince Aabir to stay in.'

'Very well, then. I'll bring the girl.'

Purohitmoshai lumbered out of the house, smiling in a manner that would have put a Cheshire cat to shame.

Chapter Eight

Pepper the Cocker Spaniel disliked forty winks. She especially disliked that time of the day when her mistresses curled up under the blankets for said forty winks, when it was clearly still daylight outside. And as far as Pepper was concerned, the presence of daylight justified ceaseless romping in the terrace garden. But once again she found tall glass panes thwarting her access to the purple crotons that she liked to pretend were enemies encroaching upon her kingdom. Pepper barked and padded into the bedroom. Like Aesop's goat, Pepper took a flying leap, but unlike the fabled goat, Pepper knew exactly where she was leaping. In the world of canine sports, Pepper would have been stiff competition for the long jump. With the precise calculations of a keen mathematician, she landed with a dull thump in the middle of the sleeping figure. As expected, the figure gave a cry.

'Pepper!'

Pepper thumped her tail in delight.

'Don't be a pest!'

Pepper continued to thump her tail.

'It's nap-time. Come sleep beside me.'

Pepper's tongue hung out in incredulity. She tried to tear away the blanket. A scuffle ensued and the figure sat up in annoyance.

'*Pepper!*'

Pepper detected anger. She continued to thump her tail, tentatively.

'I'll lock you in the bathroom, how would you like that?'

Pepper hung her head. She wouldn't like that at all.

Kimaya sighed and stretched out her hand. Pepper leapt forward gleefully. All had been forgiven!

'You're a menace,' crooned Kimaya. 'An absolute menace. We've done a really bad job of bringing you up.'

'I warned you,' said a voice at the door.

Kimaya turned around to face her mother-in-law.

'Yes you did! But I did try to insist on some discipline. I'm not the one who let her develop a taste for smoked Gouda.'

'Not hard enough. Men don't know much about bringing up anything. If I'd left Aman to my husband, he might have been a sociopath.'

Kimaya giggled. The idea of her late husband running amuck was amusing. Not that Aman hadn't been a bit of a prankster, but all in all he had been quite a brick really. Kimaya sighed. She missed him often. Large, dependable Aman, not to mention, the best looking man in the room.

'Think about The Mad Hatter,' said Tanuja Kapoor, brusquely. She lifted Pepper off the bed and smacked her bottom. Pepper yelped. 'That's for ruining our afternoon nap.'

'I'm *only* thinking about The Mad Hatter! Aman would have loved the place...especially the abundance of jam tarts. I wish I hadn't denied him tarts when he asked for them, just because I was lazy.'

'Don't beat yourself up. You didn't know a truck was going to run into him.'

Kimaya blinked. Sometimes her mother-in-law's forthrightness caught her off guard. Tanuja Kapoor was, as Kimaya's friends had commented at her wedding, a *sassy old babe*. Her pepper-salt hair was a perfect bob and her dark grey, off-shoulder dress had caused more heads to turn at the pre-wedding cocktail party than had Kimaya's own turquoise affaire. While many of her friends had waged war with their own mothers-in-law, Kimaya found that no one was more exuberant during a Ladies' Night than Tanuja Kapoor. Aman had sometimes found the need to apologize for his outrageous mother, but she knew he secretly adored her.

Kimaya often relived the night of the brutal accident that had taken Aman's life. The truck driver who had lost control of his vehicle had fled the scene, never to be found. She hadn't had the heart to harangue the police, and for once, even the irrepressible Tanuja, having lost her husband less than a year ago, had been paralyzed into a numb silence. In the grief-stricken months to follow, Kimaya had closeted herself from all company except that of her mother-in-law, and from the depths of tragedy had risen the need for pastries. Mrs and Mrs Kapoor took to baking in much the same way a jilted lover takes to the bottle. If there was a cake they liked, they baked it. The rate at which Vishnu the cook found himself buying butter and flour from the local shop, was alarming. He was further alarmed by the fact that he seemed to be getting fat, even though the women who were busy all day with mittens and whisks hadn't put on an ounce of weight!

Vishnu grumbled and swore not to touch another chocolate éclair. It was a promise made in vain of course.

And suddenly, Kimaya discovered that she was happy. The memory of her late husband had blended into the batter, resurfacing sometimes as a dull ache, but the crippling, soul-wrenching anguish had disappeared and in its place had cropped a marvellous idea—a patisserie; a dessert lounge; a *tea room*!

Tanuja was not a woman to cool her heels when an idea was waiting to be worked upon. She marched downstairs and demanded to know if the empty space was for hire. In a month she was having the floors polished and the walls painted.

'We'll call the place *Aman's*,' Kimaya had suggested.

'We can't get sentimental about business,' Tanuja had said, dismissively. 'Nobody is about to come and have tea at *Aman's*. We could be selling dhotis for all you know!'

Kimaya had laughed in spite of herself.

'*Cha-beeskoot*, like the bongs like to call it,' grinned Tanuja.

Kimaya giggled. '*Cup n Saucer*?'

'*Crème de la Crème*!'

Pepper had thumped her tail at that.

'Oooh. I do like that one,' Kimaya had grinned.

It wasn't until the floral wall paper had been picked out that Kimaya, watching *Alice in Wonderland* late one night, decided in a gleeful revelation that her little tea room was going to be called *The Mad Hatter* and nothing else.

'The Mad Hatter?' Tanuja had asked, confused.

'He has tea with the March Hare, remember?'

'Yes, I know who the Mad Hatter is, but...'

'It's my favourite Disney movie! And we can do so much

with the décor. All sorts of odd pots and pans and…oooh… the waiters can all wear dark green top hats!'

Tanuja looked amused.

'And where do you think we're going to find all these odd pots, pans and hats?'

Kimaya pursed her lips. 'I think Vic is our person.'

'Vic?'

'Vic Young. I met her a couple of years ago in London. She…'

'Oh yes, you stole her umbrella.'

'I didn't *steal*…I…' Tanuja waved her hand and Kimaya decided not to be side-tracked. 'She has a real eye for these little knick-knacks and if I can have her help me, we can have so many things shipped to us. It'll be superb, Mum!'

Tanuja had had to laugh. She had watched this young woman be forlorn too long to deny her a mad-hattered tea shop.

'Why don't you just take a trip to London and turn the place upside-down with Vic?'

'I suppose I *could*!'

And so top hats with green bow ties to match, ridiculous chinaware and seats that looked like tree stumps were dug out from all corners of the United Kingdom, with the excited and sharp-sighted Victoria Young in tow. A cookbook and six months later, *The Mad Hatter* was ready to be up and running, and Kimaya had even written the cookbook—a compilation of recipes that hadn't made the cut to be included in The Mad Hatter menu.

'Have you been to E&B yet?' asked Kimaya, absently sniffing at her cookbook. She had noticed Aabir Mookerjee sniffing at her cookbook; odd thing to do she thought. But the pages did smell good.

'That newish place on Park Street? No. But I've heard it has a good mousse.'

'I met the owner at the book launch in Tolly. He's old-fashioned, but he can't be much older than me. He seemed to be excited about Mad Hatter.'

'Bengali chap?'

Kimaya nodded.

'They're like that. Old-fashioned and excited about food.'

Kimaya snorted. Tanuja was always full of outrageous sweeping statements.

'I went to school with some Bengalis who weren't old-fashioned, but yes, they were certainly excited about food. I wouldn't want to be friends with anyone who wasn't. It's suspicious.'

Tanuja laughed too. 'I'm so hungry these days. We only ever seem to be discussing cakes and quiches. Vishnu, are there any cream biscuits?'

'There are only cream biscuits,' grumbled Vishnu. 'Everything in the house is either cream or butter or sugar.'

Kimaya chuckled. 'I believe Vishnu is beginning to look fat.'

'If he cleaned the kitchen walls twice a week like I tell him to, he wouldn't be,' said Tanuja, tersely.

'You know…I was thinking…E&B seems a nice place. I believe we could collaborate at some point of time and…'

Tanuja looked sternly over her horn rimmed glasses. 'It's too early to think of such things, Kimaya.'

Kimaya nodded and returned to her cup of green tea. She

knew when to not press a point with Tanuja. Leafing absently through her cookbook, it occurred to her that Aabir Mookerjee reeked of gentility—a quality she hadn't encountered in men her age. True, his friend Mr Raina had had the aquiline nose, but Aabir's unaffected elegance was difficult to miss. Kimaya sighed. If anything could give The Mad Hatter some much needed publicity, it was an alliance with a restaurant like E&B.

Chapter Nine

'Are you trying to tell me that there are no sweets in the kitchen?'

Purohitmoshai was exasperated at Azim's monosyllables. It was bad enough that that Aatreyee girl barely said a word, but when the servants began to emulate her, it was infuriating.

'No,' said Azim, stubbornly. He didn't see any reason to put up with this insufferable man and he wasn't going to be bullied in his own kitchen.

'Don't say lies. I know there are always sweets in this house. Do you want me to look in the fridge?'

Azim shrugged and continued to chop the okra neatly down the middle. 'Look.'

Purohitmoshai frowned. Was the man just being cheeky? He debated waddling over to the fridge, but it seemed like far too much trouble to heave himself out of the chair he had placed just in front of the garden door, so that he could see the Roys troop in. 'If this meeting turns out to be a success…' he rubbed his fat fingers in greasy glee.

Azim glared at him out of the corner of his eye. What was this man plotting again? Why did Boudi allow him to visit so much? No one liked him. Azim craned to look at the coconut tree, wondering if Aabir's grandmother was annoyed at this encroaching of territory.

'What are you looking at?' asked Purohitmoshai, his beady eyes never missing a thing.

'Thakuma,' replied Azim, shortly.

The purohit burst into a laugh that made his three chins wobble. Mukul, perched on a steel canister, looked alarmed. Thakuma would not be happy to be demeaned like this.

'Why are your eyes like saucers?' chortled the purohit.

'You are making fun of Thakuma. That is very dangerous.'

'Stop talking nonsense and get me some *mishti doi.*' Purohitmoshai was aware that any Bengali family worth its gur never ran out of mishti doi.

'There isn't any,' said Mukul, swiftly.

'Don't lie to me!' cried The Holy One, in rage. 'I shall complain to Mrs Mookerjee that you are treating me with disrespect after she has told me to make myself comfortable in the kitchen until Aabir comes home!'

'Give him some cucumber,' said Azim to Mukul.

Purohitmoshai had turned an unpleasant shade of purple. Mukul didn't like the look of it at all. Still, the man didn't deserve any of the sweets in the house, especially since Mukul and the odd-job boy liked to occasionally nibble at whatever was available.

'Aabirda doesn't like to run out of mishti doi and there's only a little left for him,' said Mukul. Azim rolled his eyes.

'Nonsense,' said the purohit. 'Aabir would be happy to let me have his curd. It's not like him to deny his guests sweetmeats.'

A snort from the door made Purohitmoshai swing around. 'You! You little monkey! How dare you!'

He tried to snatch at the odd-job boy who had been lurking outside the door, a cigarette dangling from his lips. He skipped away, laughing.

'And you're smoking! That filthy habit! Wait till I tell Debjani! Just wait!'

Azim shook his head. Many a time he had warned that stripling to not be caught smoking; nobody in the family would take kindly to it. But here he was smoking in the garden as though he were chomping on an apple.

'He might as well look for a new job now,' he muttered to Mukul. 'If Boudi hears…'

'What's that?' Purohitmoshai looked interested.

'Nothing,' said Azim.

The Holy One glowered. 'Give me some mishti doi.'

'No,' said Mukul and Azim in unsion.

A sullen silence descended on the kitchen, resonating only with the rhythmic sound of Azim's knife on the chopping board.

＄

Aabir was annoyed. It seemed that he would have to forgo his evening swim because his mother was expecting guests.

'And why am I required to entertain these nameless people tonight?' he had demanded, hotly.

'Don't be difficult, Aabir. Already my head is aching. If you add to the stress, it will only get worse. You know how my headaches never go once they come. They…'

'All right, Ma, *all right*!' said Aabir, who had no desire to hear the details of the comings and goings of his mother's headaches. He had advised less television, but as usual his advice had gone unheeded.

His mother had been suspiciously non-committal about her guests. Aabir wondered who they were and, for a moment, wondered whether he was being set up with another girl. He dismissed the thought. His mother would never have the nerve to pull off such a trick, without unwittingly letting slip her plan at some point.

Aabir broke into a tuneless hum. The apron he had ordered on a website, that seemed to specialize in all sorts of uncommon merchandize, had been delivered today. The apron itself was the colour of a red velvet cupcake, and in a font that simulated cream-cheese frosting drizzled over it, were the hilarious words—*There's much a-dough about muffin*. Aabir was rather proud of the pun and he wondered how familiar Kimaya was with Shakespeare. It struck him that the colour would complement her skin tone. He contemplated Kimaya Kapoor's skin tone for a moment and decided it was the sort of skin that one would need in order to flounce around extolling the virtues of face creams in advertisements.

He had dropped off the package, and a note that wished Kimaya luck for the grand unveiling, with the yawning guard who had been standing outside the yet unopened Mad Hatter. Aabir had avoided mentioning the apron to Rana Raina, who he had encountered strolling down the road that led to The Mad Hatter. Really, the man seemed to have simply nothing to do with his days other than stroll about on streets that led to unopened tea rooms.

'Aha!' Rana Raina had said.

'What do you mean, "Aha"?'

'What brings you to this part of town?'

'I'm always in this part of town. Some people work in this part of town.'

'E&B is *at least* ten streets away.'

'Don't be a pest.'

'What do you think of my new haircut?'

'I think nothing. I have more urgent things to do than dwell on your new haircut.'

'Like hang around outside the hot baker's house?' grinned Rana Raina.

Incorrigible. This was *exactly* why Aabir had refrained from mentioning the apron. That Raina would have made aggravating comments. He was always chock-full of aggravating comments. Aabir grimaced.

He hoped the yawning guard had delivered the apron to Kimaya before resuming his nap on his stool. Not that Kimaya had any way of contacting him really, since they had neither exchanged phone numbers nor added each other on Facebook. This Facebook business could be quite useful, thought Aabir, who often cursed all social media platforms after receiving countless messages from vague acquaintances seeking a discount at E&B.

When Aabir rolled into the driveway of Mookerjee House, he knew his mother would be agitatedly glancing out of the French windows that offered a view of the front garden from the living room. Sure enough, no sooner had he appeared at the door, than his mother leapt to her feet with a glare.

'Here he is at last! This is Aabir, my son. Poor thing always has to work late.'

'Actually I…'

But Mrs Mookerjee had cut him short.

'This is Mrs Roy and her daughter, Pragya.'

Aabir nodded at the room in general. Who in God's name were these people? He'd never seen them in his life.

'Pragya is doing her PhD at Jadavpur University,' said Mrs Mookerjee, happily. 'What did you say your thesis topic was, my dear?'

'I didn't, but I'm working to submit a conceptual framework on *Rape and its Ramifications in a Post-popian Dystopia*,' said Pragya, cheerfully.

Mrs Mookerjee choked. The girl had uttered the word *rape* in a setting such as this. Good Lord.

Aabir looked amused. 'Post-popian dystopia eh?'

'It's broadly based on Alexander Pope and "The Rape of the Lock". Except, the lock means so much more these days of course. For instance…'

'Oh I remember that,' interjected Aabir. 'Stumbled across it when I was in Oxford. Made me laugh.'

'It's hardly funny in the world we live in these days,' said Pragya, imperiously.

'Well, it wasn't for the world we live in now, was it?'

Pragya opened her mouth to argue, but her mother pressed her hand.

'Where did you study, Aabir?'

'St Xavier's, here in Cal. Then I shuttled off to Oxford to read History and Economics, though I was keen on the Classics and English course. My father thought that might be a waste of time.'

'Oh, I see. So when did you return from Oxford?'

'I taught there for a while. I've been back for a couple of years. I returned after Baba died.'

Mrs Roy nodded sympathetically and Mrs Mookerjee looked suitably melancholic.

'Do you plan to return to England now?'

Aabir's suspicions were raised at the barrage of questions. He looked at his mother, who wouldn't meet his eye.

'I'm not sure,' said Aabir, undecided.

'Pragya doesn't know if she wants to leave the country just yet,' continued Mrs Roy.

'And why would she?' asked Aabir, his mouth set in a rather thin line.

'If you decided to leave, then...'

'Oh, I won't impose my will on Pragya. I see absolutely no reason to.'

Mrs Roy looked confused.

'I think it's almost time for dinner,' said Mrs Mookerjee, hastily. 'Aabir, why don't you take Pragya out to the garden and show her that vegetable patch? She said our garden was just as she had imagined.'

Aabir spluttered. Mrs Mookerjee continued to smile benevolently.

Pragya shrugged and rose to her feet.

'What's for dinner?' glowered Aabir at his mother.

'The *paturi* will be the highlight.'

Aabir scowled. Azim had mastered the mustard-infused steamed fish that was customarily served wrapped in a banana leaf, and it was part of the standard menu for special guests. The Mookerjees had not had a special guest since Aritra Mookerjee's ashes had been sprinkled into the Ganga. Aabir was furious. Clearly, his mother could pull off a subterfuge better than he had given her credit for.

'Pumpkin,' he spat, as he stood with Pragya Roy before the vegetable patch. He could see the kitchen behind them, and outlined in the yellow light was the portly figure of Purohitmoshai. Aabir felt his cheeks become hot. That explained so much. With Thakuma's blessings, he was going to set his German Shepherd on that man.

'This garden,' said Pragya, looking around.

'Yes, yes, it is just how you imagined it to be.'

'I imagined a sprawling house like this, yes. Have you lived here long?'

'It's an ancestral home.'

'Of course. I imagine your ancestors were oligarchs who consumed the labour of the masses without offering a token reward for the sweat that was shed.'

'I beg your pardon?' responded Aabir, taken aback at this uncalled-for attack on his ancestors, wondering if the most despotic of them might indeed be eavesdropping from the coconut tree.

Pragya snorted. 'You are *such* an anglicized Bengali. To be a true Bengali is to not have a veneer of an English-educated accent.'

'But I'm not ashamed of my English-educated accent!' protested Aabir.

'Of course you're not.'

'Now look here…'

'I hear dogs barking,' interrupted Pragya.

'We have two. A Dalmatian and a German Shepherd.'

'Oh.'

'Do you not like dogs?'

'Dogs don't like me.'

Aabir raised an eyebrow. 'I think an introspection is in order.'

Pragya looked solemn for a moment. 'You don't seem to be up to this marriage business.'

'I'm not,' said Aabir, shortly.

'Neither am I, really. Besides I'm on and off with this person that my parents don't really know about.'

Aabir nodded. He thought it would be rude to ask probing questions. There was momentary silence.

'Er…' said Aabir. Was she waiting for a similar confession?

'Have you ever been soul wrenchingly in love with someone who had the power to crush you in a half-beat, and sometimes even did so?'

Taken aback, Aabir pondered the question. 'No,' he lied.

Pragya looked at him sympathetically. 'That's what it's like with this man. We have the most god-awful arguments, but no one…just no one…*gets* me like he does…you know…'

'No,' said Aabir, this time truthfully.

'And I get him too.' Pragya was on a roll. 'We're such similar people…it's amazing and terrifying…we can read the other's mind…and yet our squabbles are just blistering.'

'Ah.'

Pragya leaned against a tree. 'Maybe, I should just marry you. I can see us being friends.'

'Eh!' said Aabir, alarmed.

'And that's what a marriage should be all about. Friendship. Camaraderie. Not this soul-sucking, soul-wrenching business.'

A figure was coming down the garden. Aabir recognized his sister and waved madly.

'Hey! Hoy!'

The figure stopped.

'Hi!' cried Aabir.

Pragya looked on interestedly. Aatreyee dragged her feet towards them and came to a reluctant halt before her brother.

'Yes?'

'This is Pragya. Pragya this is my sister, Aatreyee. Pragya and her mother will be joining us for dinner,' said Aabir, glaring fiercely at his sister. She stared at him.

'I see.'

'We just met,' said Aabir, running his hand nervously through his hair, as he wiggled his eyebrows at his sister.

'We live in Golpark. I'm a PhD student in Jadavpur University. What do you do?'

'Stuff.'

Pragya looked surprised. Aatreyee turned to her brother and returned his fixed glare for a moment.

'I think there's something wrong with Churchill's leg. I

left him in your room.'

Aabir's face lit up in gratitude.

'Oh no!' he yelped. 'I must see him.' He turned to Pragya. 'I'll see you inside then.'

He raced away from marriages of camaraderie, leaving his sister with the guest.

'So,' said Pragya. 'Is that milk in that bottle you're holding?'

Aatreyee looked down at the large plastic bottle and swirled the residual milk. 'Maybe,' she said and turned back to stroll away towards the house.

Pragya observed the freshly dug earth around the vegetable patch. She slipped her foot out of a shoe and patted the damp earth. 'Have you ever been soul-crushingly, devastatingly in love with someone who's all wrong for you and yet so right?' she whispered to the pumpkin, encouraged by its stoic silence.

Chapter Ten

While arranging a wooden board that read 'Malpua Festival' outside his shop, Narayan looked up to see a familiar figure elephantining towards him. He called for a pot of mishti doi and the *malpua* to be kept ready. Purohitmoshai came to a panting halt in front of the sweet shop; one could safely assume that he was unused to walking briskly. He mopped his face with a cloth.

'Hot!' he exclaimed, eloquently. Narayan nodded sympathetically.

'Do you have any mishti doi?'

Narayan rolled his eyes. 'What sort of mithai shop runs out of sweet curd?' He signalled to his son to give the out-of-breath purohit the small meal kept aside for him.

'Cold water first,' wheezed the purohit, heaving himself into a chair. 'This malpua looks delicious,' he said, looking at the sweet pancakes rolls put before him. 'Why the sudden festival?'

'I was teaching my daughter how to make it and she made hundreds of these...used up all the milk supplies... ridiculous enthusiasm!'

Purohitmoshai chortled and dug into his sickly sweet breakfast.

'I was with the Mookerjees last night.'

'Aritra Mookerjee's family?'

'Yes. His son is so odd.'

'Really?' said Narayan, sitting down. Gossip about his patrons was one of the few things that gave him as much joy as watching the colour of warm milk turn from white to a delicious light brown as the jaggery and sugar melted into it.

Purohitmoshai nodded, with his mouth full of the mishti doi he had been craving since the previous night. 'Not that that sister of his is any better. Moves around the house like a ghost, answering in monosyllables when spoken to.'

'I heard the dead grandmother now lives on a tree.'

'That's what the servants believe. Bloody fools.'

'Are you allowed to use language like that?' asked Narayan, curiously. The Holy One shrugged.

'So what's wrong with the Mookerjee boy?'

'Refusing to get married and driving his mother hysterical.'

'That's not so odd. None of these young people want to get married.'

'He's past thirty.'

'Why is it your concern anyway?'

'His mother has given me the task of finding a suitable girl for her son.'

'Oh.' Narayan looked bored.

'And if I do…' continued the purohit, a gleam in his eye.

Narayan raised an eyebrow. 'And if you do? She's promised you an unlimited supply of butter, I suppose?'

Purohitmoshai shot his friend a withering glare. 'As much

as I would like that, there is something far better waiting for me.'

'Which is?'

The purohit moved closer to Narayan. 'There is a family heirloom. A century old emerald that Aritra Mookerjee's grandfather was presented with for saving the life of some viceroy. Hard Hinge or someone.'

'Saved life, how?'

'He was a doctor. There were riots and the viceroy got attacked. I don't really know the details. Debjani Mookerjee liked to talk about it, but that shrewish mother-in-law of hers would shut her up.'

'And she said she'll give you this emerald if you find her son a wife?' gasped Narayan.

'She did.'

'She must be really eager to have grandchildren or something.'

'She is.'

'My wife only talks about how Babloo should be married soon so we can have children again. I have no idea why. The children were such pests.' He thought of his errant daughter and his face darkened. 'Still are.'

'Who can understand women? But anyway. This son of Debjani's is turning down all the women. Probably thinks he's the King of England. Last night he left this girl stranded in the garden and ran away to play with his dog.'

Narayan guffawed.

'I'm telling you, he's a little loose up here.' The purohit tapped his forehead with a pudgy finger to indicate exactly where Aabir Mookerjee might be loose.

'In that case, best of luck with your jewel, and when you become all rich and mighty, remember your friend, the sweet-shop owner.'

Purohtmoshai heaved himself off the chair. 'If Aabir Mookerjee comes to buy curd, exalt the virtues of marriage.'

'There are none,' said Narayan, gruffly. 'None at all.'

Meanwhile, in the part of town that Calcuttans like to frequent when in the mood for a hearty meal, Aabir Mookerjee was sitting across the table at Mocambo from a woman whose shoe, he noticed, was sporting a moustache.

'That apron,' grinned Kimaya, 'was a hoot.'

'I thought so too. I was hoping you wouldn't miss the Shakespearean pun.'

'Oh, you Bengalis and your literature. No, I did not miss the Shakespearean pun. It was a good pun.'

'Wasn't it?' beamed Aabir. 'I'm going to have to take credit for that.'

Kimaya looked amused. 'So, what did you think of The Mad Hatter?'

'Quite mad. Delicious desserts. Ridiculous crockery. Where did you find those things?'

'Made a trip to the U.K. I have a friend there who has an eye for these things. She was supposed to come down for the opening of Mad Hatter, but had to postpone her trip. She should be here soon though.'

Aabir nodded. 'The top hats were a good touch.'

'Yes, you *would* like waiters in costume.'

Aabir snorted. 'Guilty as charged.' His face turned serious.

'The desserts were delicious though. Cross my heart, that crème brûlée was...'

Kimaya looked exasperated. 'Dessert, dessert! Did you even touch any of the bacon scones?'

'I think Rana Raina ate enough scones for the two of us.'

Kimaya giggled. 'Yes, he's so cute.'

Aabir pursed his lips. Women did tend to find Rana Raina 'cute'. Something about his misguided life made women want to pet him. He even had the unfair advantage of resembling a tousle-haired Lothario in a romatic comedy. In their youth, Rana Raina had left a slew of hysterical schoolgirls in his wake, especially after he took the stage by storm with a guitar and some horrendously deafening number. Aabir could never fathom what women found so alluring about a screaming man with a guitar. None of them had seemed half as frantic about his violin and he had been able to produce an impressive vibrato on third position. Aabir sighed.

'I must admit that you're not the first of your sex to have found the incorrigible Raina cute,' he said, gravely. 'I assure you though, he is far from cute. My German Shepherd, Churchill, is cute. I cannot say Rana Raina resembles him in any way.'

Kimaya exploded with laughter and the middle-aged men at the next table peered at them, curiously. For once Aabir, who abhorred drawing any sort of attention to himself, was not perturbed. He was distracted by the width of her smile. It was the kind of smile that lit up one's face and filled it with a sort of infectious joy. If Bahadur had scraped the Contessa yet again, Aabir may have let the matter pass had he been faced with that smile.

'You're a gem,' moaned Kimaya.

Aabir hoped fervently that his face was not aflame.

'I think we're going to be great friends. I should keep you around for a rainy day.'

'It was not my intention to serve as the foul-weather jester, but I'll be happy to rise to the occasion in exchange for some more of that delicious crème brûlée.'

'Of course. I'm glad you liked the crème brûlée. It used to be my husband's favourite dessert.'

Aabir blinked. 'Husband, did you say?'

'I was married. He died in a car accident.'

Aabir often found himself greatly wanting in situations that required one to be suitably sympathetic. Not that he wasn't stirred by grief, but he hadn't the foggiest how to express it. What, for instance, did one do with one's eyes? How to arrange the mouth? He mustn't appear wide-eyed, like a deer. Or slack-mouthed, like a half wit.

'I'm sorry,' he said, keeping his features perfectly arranged.

Kimaya pursed her lips. 'I'm going to let you in on a little secret.'

Aabir nodded gravely. 'I assure you I am a faithful secret-keeper. Not at all like that dastardly Pettigrew.'

Kimaya laughed. 'I love unexpected Harry Potter references. But my secret isn't half as extreme.'

'Tell me all.'

'I wrote my entire cookbook sitting in E&B.'

Aabir stared at her. 'So *that's* where I've seen you!' he exclaimed.

'I could be offended that you don't remember me,' teased Kimaya.

'In my defence, you were always huddled over a laptop. I couldn't see beyond the top of your head. And female heads are similar.'

'Not half as similar as male heads!'

Aabir waved away her objections. 'I think it's lovely that a cookbook was written in my restaurant.'

'It's the perfect place to be writing one. Delicious aromas and all that.'

Aabir beamed. 'I'll be happy to be your foul-weather jester.'

Kimaya leaned across the table, a curl coming loose from her head and falling over her eye, rather adorably he thought. No! Amusingly! Nothing adorable at all about unkempt hair. And really, what in God's name is that moustache doing on a shoe?

'Are you scoping out the competition?' she whispered, suddenly.

Aabir looked startled. 'What do you mean? Competition? Me, scoping? Of course not!'

Kimaya drew back, evidently disappointed. 'I thought you were scoping out Mocambo's menu.'

'Oh. Mocambo you mean.' Aabir's heart slackened to a more reasonable pace. 'Right. Of course, of course. I mean no, not at all, not at all.' He dug into his fish steak with gusto. She wasn't suspicious after all, of his intentions of having E&B serve heavenly crème brûlée one day.

'*What* is that thing on your shoe that looks like a moustache?' he asked, glad for a change in topic.

Kimaya laughed and waggled her white ballerina flats at him. 'It's a bow that looks like a moustache, silly.'

Aabir looked incredulous. 'I beg your pardon, I shan't for

being called silly by a woman flaunting moustached shoes!'

Kimaya shook her head. 'You're so stodgy.'

'I am no such thing. I am merely astonished at the idea of a moustached shoe.'

'Stodge. If you weren't good-looking, there would be no forgiving you.'

Aabir felt himself flaming to the roots of his hair. 'I think it is time to call for dessert,' he mumbled.

Kimaya looked amused. 'I'll skip dessert. I really need to. I'm only ever eating desserts.'

'Excellent choice,' said Aabir. 'Well, if you're going to skip dessert, I shall follow your heroic act of self-control.'

He waved to the waiter to bring the bill.

'For someone who's clearly so fond of sugar, I'm surprised you're not rolling around like a ball.'

Aabir smiled. 'I'm not a chip-off-the-old-block at all, but I did inherit some of my father's metabolism. I'm grateful for that.'

Kimaya noticed that he put down a rather handsome tip and thought that were few things more attractive than a man who wasn't likely to scrimp on a tip after he'd done himself rather well with the entrees.

Aabir led the way to the door and stepped aside when the turbaned guard held the door open for her.

'I do think that you could be an earl or something,' she quipped. 'I have a feeling that *all* your tie's crested.'

'Only some,' said Aabir, with a crooked smile. 'Once I was passed over for not being aristocratic enough.'

Kimaya stood at the entrance of Mocambo and stared at him. 'Whatever do you mean?'

'It's a story for another day,' said Aabir, lightly. 'Now my eggs and bacon beckon me. Do you need a lift home?'

'Oh no. I drove here,' said Kimaya, stepping towards a yellow Volkswagen Beetle. 'Thank you for lunch. It was such fun meeting you, Stodge.'

'Oh, so that's my name?'

'It is,' said Kimaya, closing the door of her car.

Aabir watched her drive away rather rashly, wondering why he'd mentioned the aristocratic business at all.

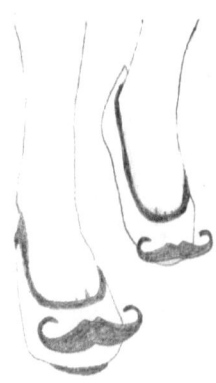

Chapter Eleven

Anjali weds Dilip. Aabir looked at the gold-and-green hued invitation and sighed. It was the wedding of the year. Weddings of the year were events that Aabir liked to avoid. Especially those that involved having to fraternize with everyone he had disliked, mildly or fervently, in school.

'Stop scowling.' Aabir felt Rana Raina's elbow dig into his ribs. His scowl deepened.

'I see Anant Tiwary looks as becoming as he used to fifteen years ago,' he said, eyeing a shaggy-haired man in a sparkling tuxedo, across the room.

'No one said money could buy a man taste or good looks. Now, try to be pleasant,' said Rana Raina, reaching for his second gin and tonic of the evening.

'Am I going to have to wheel you out on a trolley tonight?' asked Aabir.

'Please. I can totally hold my liquor. And this is why I insisted you drive tonight.'

'If you throw up in the Countess…' threatened Aabir.

'I know better than to soil that ugly old Contessa of yours. Or perhaps I should, so you can get yourself a car that was manufactured in this century.'

Aabir opened his mouth to retort, but Rana Raina cut him short. 'I see Divit Singh headed our way. Be nice.'

Divit Singh didn't look a day older than seventeen. He was still good-looking, but the spiked hair and adolescent swagger had not left him. Aabir remembered him as being too dim-witted to really be as vile as the rest of his friends.

'Hiya Aabir. Never see you anywhere.'

'Sometimes he needs a nudge,' said Rana Raina.

'Surprised to see you here too,' said Divit.

'What? Why? I'm a social butterfly!'

'You know…given the history…' Divit trailed off.

Aabir looked confused.

'Oh that,' grinned Rana Raina. 'That was a long time ago, bro. We've all moved on since then.'

Divit shrugged. 'So, where's your better half?'

'Aabir is always my better half.'

Divit smiled. 'Be like that then.'

He moved away and Aabir turned to his oldest friend, bewildered.

'History? What history? You have history?'

Rana Raina shrugged. 'I often have history.'

'What does that *mean*?' hooted Aabir.

'Anjali and I may have once been a…you know…*thing*.'

Aabir spluttered. 'And I *didn't* know? When? How? Why?'

Rana Raina yawned. 'I don't remember the details. It's been centuries. She's gotten fat since then. When I knew her, her waist was so tiny.' He held up his hands to demonstrate a tiny waist.

'You're a monster.'

'Oh please. As if you like fat women.'

'I barely *like* women, so your point is moot.'

'Stretching the truth. In kindergarten,' began Rana Raina, in a monotone that threatened to be the opening of a long-winded discourse, 'Aabir Mookerjee fell madly in love with his teacher—a pretty, young Anglo-Indian lady in floral blouses and high-heeled shoes.'

'Excuse me. I...'

'In the eighth standard,' continued Rana Raina, with his eyes half closed, 'Aabir Mookerjee felt a burning in his heart when the most-definitely gay, Mr Goswami, read aloud from *Julius Caesar* twice a week.'

'What nonsense...'

'In the twelvth standard, just before board exams, Aabir Mookerjee's infatuation, for the dimpled young thing in ochestra, soared to hitherto unknown heights when she finally smiled at him over her violin. He almost failed his finals.'

'I'm going to punch you.'

'In England, Aabir nursed his lost musical love by allowing himself to be swept off the feet by the beautiful offspring of the cousin to the heir presumptive of the Earl of Dartmouth.'

'I don't think that quite makes her a noblewoman,' said Aabir, contemplatively.

'Oh, there was nothing noble about *that* one,' said Rana Raina, shaking his head. 'Anyway. I have just successfully demonstrated that you have never liked a fat woman.'

Aabir rolled his eyes. 'Well I haven't rejected a woman outright for being fat!'

Rana Raina looked injured. 'Neither have I! I suspected Anjali made cheesecake her best friend only after we'd stopped being a…you know…*thing.*'

'I don't know why I'm still friends with you.'

'If you haven't made a girl turn to cheesecake for sustenance at least once in your life, you've been a failure.'

Aabir shook his head. 'I'm going to revel in her good fortune of not having married you.'

Rana Raina gave him a scathing look. 'Please. She's marrying for money. There are grave repercussions to that.'

Aabir spluttered. '*How* do you know that?'

'Because, essentially she's selling her soul for a Louis Vuitton?'

'You idiot. I mean, how do you know she's marrying our man, Dilip, for money?'

'Oh, I hear things,' said Rana Raina, breezily. 'Good for him though. She might be plump, but she has some excellent… you know…*skills.*'

'I don't know,' said Aabir.

'I meant, her talents lie in the…'

'*Shut up!*' hissed Aabir, alarmed that his appalling friend would be overheard, especially since the bride was approaching them.

'Rana,' smiled Anjali, looking radiant. Aabir blinked at all the transparent gemstones winking from between the folds of her orange-and-gold lehenga.

'Darling,' said Rana Raina, putting his glass down and taking the bride's hands.

'I didn't think you'd come.'

'Cancelled a trip to Delhi just for this.'

Aabir coughed at the lie.

'This is Aabir. He and Dilip were…er…friends in school.'

'We disagreed over the optimum fitting of our jeans. Dilip liked to have his hanging around his buttocks, while I liked mine firmly clasped at the naval.'

Anjali looked confused, but shot Aabir a dazzling smile anyway, before turning back to Rana Raina.

'You look gorgeous,' Rana Raina was saying. '*So* thin, you should feature in a bridal magazine.'

Aabir's jaw involuntarily went slack. Anjali giggled. 'Oh Rana. You're so full of it.'

'No, really.' He leaned in and whispered something in her ear. Blushing through her bridal make-up, she slapped his hand playfully. 'Naughty!'

'I feel like I should give you two some privacy,' said Aabir, sardonically.

'Oh, we'll catch up later, won't we?' said Rana Raina, grinning.

'Perhaps,' said the bride, coyly, and moved on to another group of guests milling around.

'Were you flirting with another man's bride?' said Aabir, fiercely.

'Nonsense. She was flirting with me. I was just letting

her. I don't want dinner here, do you?'

'Not at all. They're only serving vegetarian bilge. I think I'd like some of the fish that Azim made for lunch today. It was delicious.'

'I thought we could go to Someplace Else. The band playing tonight is one of my favourites.'

'You thought wrong,' said Aabir, rudely.

'I was going to meet Mia there.'

'Mia?'

'Meenakshi Chatterjee.'

'Good God.'

'You know, I do think that she has her eyes on you, but I'm going to turn on the Raina charm until she's blinded.'

'Do that.'

'I thought you wouldn't mind.'

'You were right.'

'Since you know…you have hot bakers to talk cake with.'

'I'm leaving.'

'Drop me off at the Park Hotel?'

'No.'

'Please! I won't mention the hot baker.'

'Fine.'

Aabir drove home after dropping off Rana Raina at the Park Hotel and refusing to accompany him inside any noisy bars. He didn't find Azim in the kitchen, but upon digging around inside the fridge, he located the left-over fish. Feeling an overwhelming urge to succumb to his Bengali roots, Aabir mixed the rice and fish together on a plate until it reached an optimum consistency and took his plate out into the kitchen garden.

'That Azim has really improved his game since I kicked the bucket.'

Aabir dropped his fish with a yelp.

'It's just me.'

'Tha…Thakuma!' cried Aabir.

'That's right.'

Aabir couldn't believe his eyes. There was his grandmother, draped in a white sari as she had been the last decade of her life, perched atop the coconut tree. Aabir had to crane his neck to really see her, but there was no mistaking that bony, straight-backed frame and glint of monocle.

'Thakuma!' he cried.

'How long are you going to cry my name?'

'But!'

'But?'

'You're…'

'Dead?'

'Yes!'

'And sitting on a coconut tree?'

'Yes!'

'And talking to you?'

'Yes!'

'It's more comfortable than you'd think.'

Aabir rubbed his neck. Staring up at the tree was giving him a crick.

'Can I scoot up to the terrace and see you?'

'Of course.'

'You won't disappear?'

'I can't promise. I must follow my ghostly instincts.'

'Thakuma!'

'All right, all right. Scoot up.'

Aabir scooted as fast as he could. On the stairs he met Churchill, who scooted with him but turned tail and ran howling as soon as he saw what was waiting on the terrace.

'That dog is such a coward,' said Thakuma, disdainfully.

'Thakuma, I must be dreaming,' said Aabir, bewildered.

'Maybe you are.'

'So, Mukul was right all these months!'

'Perhaps he was.'

'How have you been?'

'Deadly,' grinned Thakuma.

Aabir snorted. 'Can I touch you?'

'I wouldn't suggest you try.'

Aabir gaped for a moment.

'So, your mother wants you to get married?'

'Yes.'

'Don't let her force you into anything stupid.'

'Wasn't planning to, no.'

'And that fat purohit is not to be trusted.'

'I know.'

'You'll know love when it happens.'

Aabir pursed his lips. 'Will I?'

'Most definitely, yes.'

'Did you?'

'I did.'

There was a pause.

'Love doesn't exist the way it used to, Thakuma.'

'That's not true.'

'Look at the romantic comedies that are made these days. They're not romantic, and barely comic. It's such a sad reflection of our times.'

'Then you'll just have to do with the best that your times has to offer.'

There was another pause.

'Thakuma,' whispered Aabir, suddenly a little boy again, 'I'm scared to try.'

'When it happens, Aabir, it'll be a risk that you'll want to take.'

'And what if it backfires?'

'You'll pick up the pieces and move on.'

'That's easier said than done.'

'That's more commonly done than you think.'

Aabir smiled. 'You would have made a terrible kindergarten teacher.'

'I hate children.'

Aabir laughed.

'Except you. You were adorable. So like your grandfather.'

'Have you met him in the afterlife?' asked Aabir, eagerly.

'I'm not here to answer questions about the afterlife, Aabir.'

When Aabir blinked again, his grandmother was gone.

'Good night, Thakuma.'

A leaf rustled in the still night-air.

Chapter Twelve

Narayan's wife was incensed; her silver teapot was missing yet again. She thought she knew who the thief could be, but what she couldn't imagine was how it was snuck from the high cupboard that was always locked. She decided enough was enough, and it was time her husband intervened. She found him reclining in the jute hammock behind the sweet shop, fanning himself with a rolled up newspaper as he lazily chewed tobacco.

'That teapot is missing again,' said Narayan's wife, in a shrill voice. The high voice that he had found girlish and shy in his youth, seemed to be permanently raised in a shrill shriek these days. Narayan winced. It seemed he was not to be left in solitude even to sway on a hammock while he chewed on tobacco. He sighed and stopped swaying.

'Teapot?'

'The silver one.'

'What about it?'

'I can't find it.'

'Can't find the silver teapot,' said Narayan, contemplatively. His wife glared at him.

'Your daughter has it.'

'Geeta? What would Geeta do with a teapot?'

'I don't know. She likes all shiny things. Like a bird.'

'And why don't you just ask her if she has it?'

'She'll deny it. Your daughter is a thief.'

'Stop calling her *my* daughter. She's your daughter too. In fact, you had her for a whole nine months before I set eyes on her.'

Narayan's wife looked as if she might break into another shriek. He rolled out of his hammock hurriedly.

'Okay, okay. What do you want me to do?'

'Tell her to stop stealing all our things. I think we should just marry her off.'

'If she's going to steal her husband's things, he might beat her to death.'

'I think she *should* be beaten. Spoilt brat. Stealing my silver teapot.'

'I'll go talk to her.'

'And ask her how she got it from a locked shelf when I have the key with me all the time.' Narayan's wife swung the set of keys tied to the end of the pallu of her sari. Narayan sidestepped to avoid any swinging keys. His wife shrieked again.

'What? *What?*'

'The kitchen keys are missing.'

'There you go. Someone has the key.'

'That girl! You go talk to her. Talk to her right now!'

'Fine. *Fine.*'

121

Narayan stormed off towards the house in his search of his daughter. He found her on the terrace, massaging hot coconut oil into her long hair.

'Your mother is missing her silver teapot.'

She looked at him nervously and began to braid her well-oiled hair.

'Have you got it?'

'I just wanted to look at it.'

'Why do you take her things without telling her?'

'She won't let me have them if I asked,' said Geeta, sulkily.

'But how did you open the cupboard?'

'I just did.'

'Geeta.' Narayan looked stern.

'I took the key from her pallu when she was sleeping. I just wanted to look at the teapot. It's pretty.'

'Then you should have looked at it and kept it away.'

'But I heard dada coming in and got scared, so I shut the cupboard and went to my room.'

'Give me the keys and the teapot.'

'Okay.'

Narayan turned to follow his daughter to her room. He watched her fingers lightly sweeping the banisters as she tripped down the stairs, and he stopped for a moment. He had had an idea.

Aabir Mookerjee grimaced. If there was anything that disoriented him more than a mall, it was a noisy mall. It seemed that most people were wont to bellow across stores while children these days were given to believe that the world was their playground. A yowling toddler scampered around his legs as her older brother chased her, brandishing what looked to be a hairclip. Aabir scowled after them, berating himself for having ruined a Sunday morning in an exercise in futility. Procuring a birthday gift for his sister was by far one of the most challenging chores on his annual to-do list. Though his friends and family shared similar sentiments about his own birthday when it rolled around, unlike Aabir, they had no qualms about handing him crisp cash, enclosed in comical cards that he thought were inane.

Aabir strongly believed that money should exchange hands only as charity or a professional transaction; birthdays especially were no occasion for financial remuneration. He had thus spent more than a decade attempting to find his sister a gift that met her impossible strictures. He had dug up obscure books, but somehow she'd got her hands on them already. Twice she had accepted elegant stationery with a half-smile, but had never worn the beautiful pearl brooch or the houndstooth scarf, and had even given away the green leather handbag that Aabir had overheard her admiring on her friend.

His mother had sniffed, in a patronizing I-told-you-so way that always got Aabir's hackles up.

'I *heard* her telling that Saira girl that the green bag looked great!' he had exclaimed.

'Doesn't mean a thing. You pretended to like that striped tie I gave you three years ago and I've never see you wear it. Actually,' his mother looked up thoughtfully, 'was Raina's son wearing it the other day?'

Aabir had coloured. It was true. He had given away that

123

tie to Rana Raina, who was fairly non-discerning about his clothes.

'I'd liked the cobalt blue, Ma, with alice-blue stripes.'

'That's what you got. Blue tie with bue stripes.'

'Er...not quite...what you gave me was an azure tie with periwinkle stripes.'

Mrs Mookerjee had shaken her head sadly at twenty-one-year-old Aabir. She had thought to herself that her children may have inherited their grandmother's madness, but there was no one she could voice her fears to, not while Thakuma was still alive and wielding her iron hand at any rate!

Now that that time of the year had crawled back again, Aabir found himself wandering aimlessly around the mall. He stopped in front of a mannequin sporting a very large sun-hat. Not that Aatreyee needed protection from the sun, he thought. She was already a ghostly white. Some sun, in fact, would do her a world of good. He turned away and came up face-to-face with a grinning figure.

'Aha!' said the grinning figure.

'Hello there. Are you a ghastly weekend shopper? If so, I'm afraid our infant friendship must end here.'

'What are you babbling about? Of course our infant friendship must end here. I have caught you in the midst of your dirty little secret.'

Aabir looked surprised. Kimaya Kapoor pointed accusingly at the sun-hatted mannequin at the window. 'Were you or were you not ogling the mannequin in the gold bikini?'

Aabir swung around and gaped. It was true. The mannequin was flaunting its impossibly thin body in a gold bikini.

'Bik...' he stuttered, 'oh no...it was the sun-hat...I wasn't...'

Kimaya Kapoor seemed to be revelling in Aabir's discomfiture. A child crawled between Aabir's feet, clutching a lollypop. He drew himself to his full height and faced Kimaya squarely. 'Madam, I assure you that I am *not* in the habit of ogling mannequins, in bikinis or otherwise. I generally refrain from harassing women, whether they're of flesh and blood or fiberglass and paint.'

Kimaya chewed her lip thoughtfully. 'I might have to give you the benefit of the doubt,' she said. 'Mostly because this infant friendship is endless entertainment.'

'Oh, is that what you think?'

'That's exactly what I think.'

Aabir surveyed her askance. His gaze stopped at an interesting hair accessory. 'You're hairclip. It's like the keys of a piano.'

Kimaya shook her long pony-tail. 'It's new. A friend of mine just flew down from London. She brought me this.'

'You wear some of the oddest things I've ever seen on an individual,' said Aabir. 'Newspaper skirts…moustached shoes…piano-key hairclips.'

'Noticed, did you?' grinned Kimaya.

'Couldn't help but,' retorted Aabir, recovering quickly from the brink of an embarrassing moment.

'I'm going to take that as a compliment,' said Kimaya. 'What are you doing here, if you're not ogling mannequins in bikinis?'

Aabir let out an exasperated sigh. 'My sister is the bane of my existence!'

'A sister? This is the first time you've mentioned her.'

'Because she's a bane!'

'Why is she a bane?'

'Impossible to pick out a darned gift for her. Her birthday is a trying time for me.'

Kimaya giggled. Aabir scowled at her. 'Are you being endlessly entertained again?'

'Sort of.'

'Cease to be.'

'All right, all right. Give her a perfume.'

'She won't use it. Persnickety about fragrances.'

'Persnickety,' repeated Kimaya thoughtfully. 'Charming word. That's what I want to call you.'

'You're already calling me Stodge.'

'I like Persnickety better. What about pearls? A single strand. Can't go wrong.'

'Did once. The pearls were too round, I believe.'

'A funny umbrella?'

'I'll find *you* one.'

'You must! I think funny monsoon accessories are the best. Anything to cheer up a gloomy day. I hate rain!'

'So do I!' exclaimed Aabir. 'Mud. Traffic. Flooding. The third world is just not equipped to handle monsoon!'

'I wonder if that's a politically incorrect thing to say.'

'Hogwash. Political correctness is overrated.'

Kimaya stopped their meanderings to consider a pair of high-heeled pumps at the shop window.

'I needed a pair of red pumps, you know. I like this dark-red colour.'

'Well it's more auburn than dark red, if you know what I mean,' said Aabir, peering at the shoes.

Kimaya stared at him.

'Took a great interest in colours as a child,' shrugged Aabir.

'You surprise me every day,' said Kimaya. 'I think I actually like you.'

Aabir was surprised that the confession made him inordinately pleased.

Kimaya was moving down the marbled corridor of the mall. 'I'll stop by later. When we're not pondering what to get your mysterious sister.'

'Oh, are we doing that?' said Aabir, catching up with her. 'Don't you have to be somewhere?'

'I only stopped by the supermarket for this cream cheese,' replied Kimaya, patting the paper bag in her hand. 'I'm expecting my friend to join me for lunch. Have sent the car back for her and have some time to kill. Do you think an English rose will like that new Afghani joint?'

'English rose, is she? I knew an English rose once, who abhorred Indian food and its spices and general messiness.'

'How boring of her. Who was she?'

'A dear friend,' said Aabir, not averting his eyes from the rows of glass windows they were strolling by.

Kimaya grunted. 'This particular English rose once had a fling with an Indian man. So I think Afghani food should be a success.'

'If you say so.'

Kimaya squinted at him and then decided she didn't want to probe.

'I suppose you're not the kind to just give someone money on their birthday.'

Aabir looked at her, surprised. 'No, I'm not,' he agreed. 'I wish my mother would stop badgering me to. I think it's in exceedingly bad taste. And I never know what's too much or too little, so I run the risk of being eccentric or tight-fisted.'

'Your sister will know you're not tight-fisted and I'm sure she's familiar with your eccentricities. But yes, I get that it's not your thing.'

'Yes, it's not my...*thing*.'

'She likes books?'

'Of course. But I nearly always give her something she's already read or doesn't like.'

Kimaya raised an eyebrow. 'That's quite a library she must have, then.'

'We do have a sizable library, yes. I've been meaning to get it arranged. Books lying around, all higgledy piggledy. And Aatreyee—my sister—loses her mind when she thinks someone's borrowed a book and hasn't returned it. She used to hound my friends in school. Very embarrassing. Not that I approve of books not being returned, but...'

Kimaya clutched his arm in excitement. 'I have it!'

'What, what?'

Kimaya bounced on the balls of her feet.

'What have you got?' asked Aabir, impatiently.

'Have you ever been to a library?'

Aabir gave her a withering look.

'Of course, you have,' babbled Kimaya. 'So, those stamps they use to date the book? You know...blue ink...'

'Indigo.'

'I'll kill you.'

'I'm sorry. Nasty habit.'

'Yes it is. So those stamps. There's a place in the basement of this mall that makes personalized stamps! She can stamp all her books! We'll think of something cool to say…oh come *on…*'

Aabir's scepticism started to give way. This did seem to him a darned good idea.

'The enigma should at least be amused! Right?'

'The who?'

'Enigma. Your sister.'

Aabir chuckled. 'You could call her that.'

'Persnickety and Enigma. I should write a children's book.'

'Only after we have procured this stamp.'

'Oooh yes. What shall it say? "Hands will be chopped off if due date is not met".'

'Not quite so bloody perhaps.'

'This book comes to life if not returned by the due date.'

'Aatreyee Mookerjee's library. Borrow at your own peril.'

129

Kimaya chewed her bottom lip. 'Yes, I think you're right. That's it.'

Aabir beamed. Kimaya looked at her phone vibrating in her hand. 'Hey, the English rose has arrived. I'll see you later? Well actually…join us for dinner?'

'Oh no, I wouldn't want to intrude.'

'Don't be an ass. I wouldn't be inviting you if it was going to be an intrusion, would I?'

'Your argument is infallible,' said Aabir, thoughtfully.

'Good. Skip up to the third floor after you're done purchasing the stamp.'

Kimaya herself skipped down the escalator and found her English rose waiting hesitantly by the revolving doors of the mall. She was evidently disconcerted by the number of men who did a double take as they passed her by or by the number of men who passed her by just to do a double take. Victoria Young was undoubtedly beautiful; the sort of beauty that made men involuntarily do a double take. It is not a matter of surprise then that her golden hair—that particular shade of gold, one suspected, had driven Porphyria's lover quite mad—and peach dress which, for all its simplicity, emphasized an impossibly slender frame, had garnered a morbid interest amongst the kind of men who liked to loaf around the mall in summer, simply to avoid the oppressive Calcutta heat. Their morbid interest made Victoria blush, which she did rather prettily, averting her blue eyes to consider the height of the ceiling. It is in this stance that Kimaya found her, as she stepped off the escalator.

'Turning your nose up at us brown people, are you?' she grinned.

Victoria was startled. 'Oh, no. I was only trying to avoid having to look at those boys there. They seem to find me as fascinating as a one-legged elephant.'

Kimaya swung around and shouted something rude that made Victoria wince even though she hadn't understood a word.

'Uncouth bastards. I suppose the drive here was all right? Durgesh is about the best we've hired in years.'

'Er…yes…he driving was beyond reproach, am sure…'

'I suspect a *but*.'

'It's unspeakably crowded!' exclaimed Victoria. 'I was petrified the whole time that a bus was simply going to mow us down while changing lanes. Or we'd just run over a pedestrian…why do they just *dash* across the road like that?! It could be fatal!'

'Often is,' said Kimaya, cheerfully.

Victoria looked horrified. 'And an…an *armless* man knocked on my window and sort of waved his…his stump at me. I screamed. And your chauffeur waved him away. But… an *armless* man…'

Kimaya chuckled. 'Entertaining drive for Durgesh, am sure.'

Victoria stopped short.

'There are just so many people here!' she exclaimed. 'It's all of Sussex in a mall, I suspect.'

Kimaya clutched the banisters and laughed. 'Oh God, this visit is going to be full of epiphanies. They're not lying, you know, when they say India's population is out of control. Remind me to point out a bus during rush hour.'

'I think this heat has sapped me of all appetite.'

'The Afghani buffet is going to revive it again.'

'Afghani, did you say?'

'Yes. Delicious kababs. A friend of mine is going to join us. He's a riot. You'll like him. Used to live in London once too. Oh here he is.'

Kimaya waved to catch the approaching Aabir's eye. It was only at about ten feet away that he stopped short, meeting the aghast blue eyes of Victoria Young. The whole world swam before him.

Chapter Thirteen

Purohitmoshai was displeased. Even the large pot of mishti doi had not wiped the scowl off his face.

'Where is your father?' he growled to the lanky boy standing in front of him. 'Why has he asked to see him at this time of the day when all respectable Brahmins are catching their afternoon nap?'

Babloo looked at the clock as it struck three and was amused.

'What are you grinning at like a goat?' snapped the purohit.

'Nothing, nothing,' said Babloo, hastily. 'Baba will be with you soon.'

'What do you mean *soon*?' asked the purohit, irritably. 'How soon is *soon*?'

'Soon is now,' said Narayan, coming out from the shop to the backyard behind it. 'You're so bad tempered during the day!'

'You woke me up and insisted I see you. Why couldn't you see me?' said the purohit, plaintively.

Narayan waved his son away and sat down on the bench next to the purohit. Babloo gave them a curious look and moved away.

'Because I have a business to run,' said Narayan, lighting a cigarette. 'Now listen to me. I have a brilliant idea that will help you *and* me.'

The purohit frowned. 'What is it?'

'My daughter has nimble fingers.'

Purohitmoshai stared at the sweet-shop owner, confused. 'I see.'

'She also has a knack for opening locked cupboards.'

'Are you calling your daughter a thief?' spluttered the purohit.

'She could be, yes.'

The Holy One dug a spoon into the sweet curd. 'What's your idea?' he asked, cautiously.

'Find her a place at the Mookerjees. Once she's inside, she'll be able to find the emerald very quickly and then she'll bring it to us. But we have to share the profits.'

Purohitmoshai pursed his lips.

'I'm risking my own daughter,' said Narayan. 'If she gets caught...'

'I can get her in, but I can't guarantee her safety,' said the purohit. 'If she gets caught, I won't take any responsibility.'

Narayan considered for the first time, perhaps, that he didn't really like this podgy man of God. Still...compromises must be made if one was on the brink of making a fortune.

'She won't get caught,' he said, shortly. 'She never gets caught.'

'Been practising thievery, has she?'

Narayan resented the sneer on The Holy One's face. He watched him scraping out the hardened cream from the sides of the earthen pot with some disdain.

'I'll see what can be done,' said Purohitmoshai, sitting back with a burp. 'Mind you, don't think you can run away with the stone once she's given it to you.'

Narayan stiffened. 'I wasn't planning to.'

'Glad we made that clear.' Purohitmoshai staggered to his feet with a yawn. 'I'll drop in when I've had a word with Debjani Mookerjee.'

❧

When Aabir Mookerjee left London to move back to India after his father's bereavement, he had prepared himself to never revisit some of his favourite habits—hunting down hidden little tea shops in search of pastries, habitually losing himself in the labyrinth of the London underground and Victoria Young.

Victoria was a drug that had taken him more than a year to be weaned off. The withdrawals had been painful. Rehabilitation had taken its time; Eggs and Bacon had worked its miracle. But none of that had prepared him for this chance encounter with the English rose, *his* English rose, in the middle of his sweaty, crowded city. He knew now that Macbeth had not overreacted at all when he'd caught sight of Banqo's ghost.

'What's the matter with the two of you?' said Kimaya, surprised. 'What am I missing here?'

'I think it would be difficult for me to summarize that in this very moment, my dear,' murmured, Victoria. She stepped forward and smiled, uncertainly.

'How unexpected,' she said.

'You don't say,' said Aabir, recovering a little. He realized with a pang that he was in in an old pair of leather loafers—the ones he saved for running errands in. His striped shirt was non-descript; the stripes were definitely two millimetres broader than he liked them to be. He felt suddenly savage towards his mother. If she would just stop *giving* him clothes, he could stop feeling obliged to wear them.

'You look the same, Aabir.'

'And you look...well...quite beautiful really. As always.'

Kimaya cleared her throat. Aabir jumped.

'Oh, how rude of me! Kimaya, this is Victoria...' he hesitated, 'from London.' He turned back to Victoria. 'Where are you putting up, by the way?'

Victoria giggled.

'At my house,' said Kimaya, a trifle coldly. 'We're friends, you know.'

Aabir's eyes widened. 'It's a small world. I had no idea you two knew each other.'

'We met a couple of years ago. She'd run off with my umbrella,' said Victoria, laughing. 'Then she tracked me down and returned it. Remember how you used to pull my leg for pinning my address on nearly everything I owned.'

'An absurd and dangerous habit,' said Aabir.

'Well, I found my umbrella and gained a friend.'

'How do you two know each other?' asked Kimaya, squinting at Aabir, whose face had become vaguely stiff after the initial shock of seeing Victoria Young. 'We...met in Oxford. She used to study History of Art, while I was doing Economics.'

'We had a common literature class,' said Victoria, looking the most animated Kimaya had seen her since she'd landed on foreign shores. 'We disagreed over P.G. Wodehouse. Aabir thinks the man is a genius.'

'Victoria thought he was borderline ridiculous and that made me angry.'

Was that a glow in his eyes, thought Kimaya. She shrugged. 'Lunch anyone?'

'Oh right. Er...Afghani food,' said Victoria.

A thought struck Kimaya. 'Is this the English rose you once knew who didn't like Indian food?' she asked Aabir.

Aabir smiled. 'Yes, it is. Not that Afghani food is strictly *Indian*, but you know what I mean.'

'I would prefer something a little less spicy I think,' said Victoria. 'Food from the Subcontinent has a way of burning a hole in my stomach.'

'Oh, fine. I'll just take you to Aabir's snooty little place. It's called Eggs and Bacon. You'll probably like that.' Kimaya was annoyed at this unexpected change of plans. Not that she was a stickler for plans, she mused. She wasn't...*persnickety* like that at all.

Aabir hadn't noticed that this was the first time Kimaya had used his name. Something discomforting had just occurred to him; the passing jibe that Kimaya had made about how her visiting friend had once had a fling with an Indian man. Fling. The word gnawed at him now, causing a little hollow in his stomach and feeling its way rather uncomfortably up his innards. Aabir didn't feel like lunch.

'I don't think I'll join you,' he said. 'But I hope you like my little place.' He swung around and walked briskly towards the exit that led to the mall parking lot. Kimaya stared after him.

'Eggs and Bacon,' murmured Victoria.

Chapter Fourteen

When Purohitmoshai arrived at Mookerjee House, he found that the good lord had made his job easier for him; Mrs Mookerjee was in the process of flinging yet another object at the odd-job boy. The object, a tin of roasted peanuts this time, missing its grinning mark by a few yards, landed with a dull thud at the purohit's feet. The lid flew open and roasted peanuts rolled out of their confinement rather excitedly. As if on cue, Churchill came bounding in to view. Unexpected treats were even better than scheduled evening walks. Mrs Mookerjee looked at him in disgust. Why were dogs always so *greedy*?

'Why are you so worked up?' asked Purohitmoshai, looking askance at Churchill and hurriedly stepping out of his way.

'This useless boy. All he had to do was go to the cake shop and collect the cake that I had ordered, and somehow he has bungled that up!'

The Holy One shook his head at the odd-job boy. 'Why are you laughing? Is this funny to you?'

The odd-job boy's grin widened even though panic was beginning to register in his eyes. It had always been a problem;

when he got into trouble he was unable to stop his lips from forming this hideous grin and had been beaten many a time by his irate father.

'Fool!' shrieked Mrs Mookerjee. She wrung her hands. 'It's my daughter's birthday and it's so difficult to get her anything she likes. I know she loves this dense chocolate cake that needs to be pre-ordered. And now this stupid boy has gone and brought back someone else's strawberry cream cake!'

'I've been telling you for a long time,' said the purohit, gravely, 'to fire that good-for-nothing. I have someone very reliable willing to work for you.'

'Who?' asked Mrs Mookerjee, eagerly. Servants that came recommended were a weakness. If she could, she would have collected them like sarees.

138 'Narayan's daughter is looking for a job. He doesn't want to let her go work in just any house, but I know he thinks very highly of your family.'

'The sweet-shop owner?'

'Yes. Very hard-working daughter he has. Clever too.'

'I don't like them to be too clever,' said Mrs Mookerjee, doubtfully. 'Then they cause problems.'

'Oh, she's not too clever at all. Sometimes she can be quite stupid,' said Purohitmoshai, anxiously. 'But she's clever in the kitchen and around the house.'

Mrs Mookerjee looked thoughtful. The purohit looked at the pink-and-white icing on the cake that lay on the table in the open box. 'Think of how disappointed your daughter will be. Birthdays happen only once a year.'

'You're fired,' snapped Mrs Mookerjee at the dismal figure in the corner.

The odd-job boy grinned widely.

❦

Upstairs, Aabir Mookerjee sat unseeingly at his writing desk. E&B paperwork lay before him, but the concentration he generally employed for the perusal of important documents was now employed for the act of wool-gathering. It wasn't just ordinary wool that he was gathering either; it was long-forgotten wool, wool that he liked to seldom visit. Like his grandmother, Aabir Mookerjee did not agree with the notion that hearts should be worn on sleeves. He was of the stoic opinion that the heart belonged within its membranous pericardium and any irrational contractions were not for all to witness. Victoria Young had once witnessed the irrational mechanisms of Aabir's heart. He winced now as he recalled letters that would put a Shakespearean sonnet to blush, pink roses that had made his favourite florist all the richer, days that were golden even when they'd been grey. Picnics in gardens... skipping class to curl up in the library together...midnight walks in search of hot buns...his young Victoria. How they had laughed when the movie starring Emily Blunt had hit the theatres.

When it had all ended, he had been almost glad that his father's death had brought him back to his own country. He hadn't been prepared for the end. He hadn't foreseen an end. Neither, she claimed, had she. He had believed her then, but now he wasn't so sure. The door opened and Lady Mountbatten led her mistress in.

'I knocked,' said Aatreyee.

'Oh, I didn't hear,' said Aabir, rummaging around his

desk. He found the little red package and held it out. 'Happy Birthday.'

She raised an eyebrow and began to meticulously tear away the cellotape that held it, without ripping the paper. This was a habit Thakuma had insisted her grandchildren inculcate. 'People have taken the time and effort to make their gift look nice. If you can't respect that, you don't deserve a gift,' she had told a tearful Aabir, while taking away his toy-train because he had torn up the wrapping paper in all his enthusiasm.

Aatreyee looked curiously at the stamp. Aabir found a book he'd borrowed from her and opened it to the first page. 'Stamp it.'

Aatreyee Mookerjee's library. Borrow at your own peril. Aatreyee's face lit up and she laughed. Aabir looked at her in delight; she looked like a different person when she was chose to smile. 'Do you like it?'

'Wicked!'

'Is that a good thing? A cool friend of mine told me about it!'

'Thanks, Dada.'

Aabir grinned. She rarely called him that, acknowledging his big-brother status. She rarely called him anything.

'See you at lunch,' Aatreyee turned to leave the room.

'Wait. What did you come in to tell me?'

Aatreyee stopped. 'There's no cake.'

'What do you mean *no cake*?'

Aatreyee shrugged. 'Ma said so.' She left the room while her brother frowned. In the Mookerjee House, it wasn't a birthday if there was no cake. And it wasn't a cake if it wasn't chocolate.

He trotted down the stairs and found Purohitmoshai occupying a good part of an ample couch. Aabir's frown deepened.

'Aabir,' said Purohitmoshai, breaking into a smile. 'How are you? What have…'

'Where's Ma?' asked Aabir, shortly. Why must his mother entertain this phony so often?

'Trying to find your sister a birthday cake.'

'What happened to the one we ordered?'

'The boy brought home the wrong cake. It was pink.'

Aabir shuddered. He could imagine just the sort of Gelusil-pink cream that had been used as frosting. 'Then send him back for the right one!'

'Do you think I didn't try that?' cried Mrs Mookerjee, appearing behind Aabir. He jumped. 'The shop said they'd put both boxes down on the counter so we must have picked up the wrong parcel. It's not their fault. They gave me the number of the horrible cream-cake buyer.'

'And?'

'The woman was very rude. She said she lived too far and wasn't going to travel just to return the cake. She hung up before I could offer to pick it up and hasn't answered my calls since.'

'Of course she won't. She has a delicious chocolate cake instead of a vile pink one.'

'I've fired him.'

'Fired who?'

'That boy.'

'What!' Aabir did not approve of his mother's habit of firing the help. He insisted that good work could be coaxed from most people with the right attitude and incentives. Mrs Mookerjee disagreed. Once a bad worker, always a bad worker, she liked to argue.

'He deserved it.'

'Fine. See if you can find another reliable help.'

'I already have! Purohitmoshai knows someone.'

Aabir groaned inwardly. This could only mean trouble. 'I hope then that his recommended help is more suitable than his brides.'

Purohitmoshai scowled and his mother glared at her son. 'What are we doing about the cake?' she asked him, sternly. 'Should we risk another kind of chocolate cake?'

'I'll look into it,' said Aabir, leaving the room, but not before he'd shot the purohit a look of distaste.

Upstairs, he contemplated calling Rana Raina. If there was anyone who could pull strings to procure a cake that wasn't available off the counter, it was him. But before that he had an important call to make. If one was going to be rude and simply stalk away from lunch plans, then the least one could do was be apologetic about it.

Kimaya Kapoor's phone rang for a long time before she answered it.

'Hi.' She sounded curt.

'I suppose I'm intruding on an elaborate Saturday afternoon brunch.'

'There isn't any time for elaborate Saturday afternoon brunches,' was her crisp reply.

'Such is the ironic life of a restaurateur.'

'Yes.'

'I'm afraid I behaved rather badly yesterday. I didn't mean

to be rude,' said Aabir, buckling down to unpleasantries. 'I'm awfully sorry...' He trailed off anxiously when he heard a sigh.

'No, I don't think you did mean to be rude. It was all a little unexpected. Vic has been out of sorts too. And I can only guess what this is all about.'

'I'll explain someday.'

'No, it's none of my business. Hey, did your sister like the stamp?'

'Oooh, she was thrilled! I can't thank you enough.'

'So I've achieved the impossible?'

'I would certainly say so. But now our odd-job boy has been fired for bungling up the cake, so it's absolute mayhem here.'

'Buy her another cake.'

'She liked this particularly dense, dark-chocolate cake from Kookie Jar, but it needs to be pre-ordered.'

'I know a place where you can get a dense, dark-chocolate cake, which I'm sure Enigma would love.'

'Where?' asked Aabir, eagerly.

'This new joint called The Mad Hatter. It's supposed to be good.'

Aabir laughed. 'You've truly saved this day. Shall I swing by in half an hour?'

'I'll leave it at the counter,' said Kimaya.

Aabir frowned. Was she avoiding meeting him?

'And thanks for lunch yesterday. Your maître d' didn't let us pay.'

'Least I could do,' said Aabir, swallowing the urge to ask if Victoria had enjoyed herself. If her old mood swings still prevailed though, she had probably moped all through dinner and skipped dessert, something Aabir used to find terribly disconcerting. He hung up and was surprised to find himself humming an old tune. It wasn't, in fact, a song that reminded him of the Victoria days; it was a song from *Beauty and the Beast* that had been playing in the background of The Mad Hatter's opening night.

Chapter Fifteen

Tanuja Kapoor eyed the young women over her bowl of chopped watermelon. She grimaced when she discovered that the fruit was not half as sweet as she would have liked it to be and pushed her bowl away. Pepper's head swung around to follow the movement of the bowl across the table, but she decided she was far too comfortable having her ears fondled by this new addition to the household. Pepper had taken to Victoria ever since she'd stepped through the door. She smelt different, but certainly like someone who knew how to tickle a belly. And that was always the hallmark of the Right Kind of Person.

Kimaya was lying on her sofa, gazing out at the sunny clouds, looking not particularly sunny herself. Tanuja narrowed her eyes at her. The girls had returned from the mall that evening, rather low in spirits and hadn't been particularly cheerful since. Tanuja was not one to pry into the affairs of young people—a philosophy that had made her 'the coolest mom' on the block—but she couldn't help wondering what had curbed Kimaya's exuberance. She had been looking forward to Victoria's cutting-edge ideas for The Mad Hatter and yet nothing mad at all was being planned. Tanuja cleared her throat.

'Why are you two moping around the house today?'

Victoria turned around languidly. 'Moping?' she smiled. 'Is that what we're doing?'

'Looks like moping to me,' said Tanuja, brusquely.

'We have plans this evening. Flurys for tea.'

'I see. And what about The Mad Hatter?'

'It's catching on. The crème brûlée is doing well.'

'It really is an excellent crème brûlée,' said Victoria.

'Thanks.'

Kimaya didn't tear her gaze away from the window. Tanuja sighed and rose slowly to her feet; her arthritis wasn't getting any better.

'I'm meeting the girls at Tolly in an hour. I hope you two find yourselves something to do.'

She leaned over to ruffle Pepper's head, like she did just as she was about to leave the house, and left the room. The slamming of the front door made Kimaya wince.

'Are you moping?' she asked, tearing her eyes away from the sunny sky. She blinked as the room turned dark for a moment.

'Not…particularly,' said Victoria, uncertainly.

'Is Aabir the Indian dude you were telling me about? The one you had a fling with?' Kimaya decided she had had enough with beating around the bush.

'Yes, though it was a trifle more serious than a fling.'

'I gathered,' said Kimaya, sardonically. 'That was the face of a man who had seen a ghost.'

Victoria spread herself languidly on the couch and

protested when Pepper tried to clamber on her.

'Pepper!' said Kimaya, sharply.

Pepper took it as a sign to bound over. A flying leap later, she was on Kimaya's stomach.

'You're really not a feather-weight anymore,' grumbled Kimaya, as Victoria giggled. Pepper thumped her tail and Kimaya obliged her by tickling her neck, just as she'd been trained to do.

'I miss my Corgis at home already,' sighed Victoria.

'Corgis? How royal of you.'

Victoria smiled. 'I suspect my father *was* taking a leaf out of the queen's book when he brought home those two. They're even called George and Henry.'

Kimaya laughed. 'Oh lord. I'd be surprised if the queen had named any of *her* Corgis after respectable ancestors.'

'Aabir used to get along with them famously,' said Victoria, suddenly. 'I think they still miss him. Sometimes they sniff at the pocket square he left behind and look around unhappily.'

'What kind of pocket square?' asked Kimaya, curiously. It seemed to be a pertinent question.

'Blue with white polka dots,' replied Victoria, absently.

'True blue? Oxford blue? Teal?'

'What?' Victoria looked confused.

'Nothing, nothing. Carry on.'

Victoria pursed her lips. Kimaya thought it was unfair how beautiful she looked simply reclining on the couch, but quelled the uncharitable jealousy that was beginning to well up.

'I'll have to admit, I did wonder whether I'd see him. I knew his home was Calcutta, but I didn't know if he still lived here.'

Kimaya said nothing, hoping her silence would encourage Victoria to keep talking.

'You see, when we broke it all off, I didn't hear from him at all, except a brief email to inform me that he'd be moving back to India,' continued Victoria slowly. 'And I didn't reply.'

Kimaya didn't say anything. Even Pepper lay very still.

'I didn't know what to say. Or how to say what I wanted to say. And soon it was too late to say anything.'

Victoria sighed.

'Why...?' asked Kimaya, hesitantly.

'He...my father...he wasn't...'

'He wasn't British?'

Victoria shook her head rather miserably. 'You see Kimaya...my father isn't an aristocrat really, but his cousin is about to be the Earl of Dartmouth. He wants me to make a...a strategic marriage...so that...'

'I see,' said Kimaya, astonished. 'Poor Aabir.'

'Yes,' said Victoria, sitting up, her blue eyes flashing. 'Poor Abe. Poor dear Abe. He should never have got himself involved with that British bitch!'

She stormed out of the room and Kimaya heard a door slam. Pepper yelped in protest. Why couldn't everyone just be peaceful?

◦───◦

After wrapping things up at E&B that evening, Aabir crossed the road to Flurys instead of simply walking down Park Street to the Calcutta Club, as was his habit. He had received a cryptic message from Kimaya that had informed him to make himself available at that famed confectionery. Aabir, who had always been of the opinion that intuition did not belong exclusively to the female species, was fairly certain that this had something to do with his former girlfriend. He was therefore much better prepared for this encounter, shod in his favourite oxblood brogues and lucky argyle socks. He tried to ignore the dampness of his palm as he stepped inside Flurys and looked around for a familiar face.

When his eyes fell on Victoria, she was turned away from him. Aabir paused for a moment to soak in the déjà vu that enveloped him. There she was, bent over a book, a finely manicured hand wrapped around a cup of tea, golden hair swept to one side, leaving the nape of her neck bare. In a moment Aabir was transported back to the little tea room off Leicester Square, that fateful afternoon when his quest for blueberry scones had opened up a whole new world to him. The world of Victoria Young.

When Victoria looked up and her blue eyes smiled at him even before her lips had parted, a number of men were transfixed. Standing in the middle of Flurys however, Aabir realized that after all these years of chuckling at Wilde's irreverence, he was now staggering under the influence of that particular device that humourists liked to call bathos.

Bathetic, thought Aabir and fought to keep a straight face at his own wit. But as Victoria continued to gaze at him, he began to feel almost ashamed at his inability to feel the goosebumps he had been expecting and the rush of memories that should have come flooding. He noticed instead that his hands were no longer clammy and his pulse had miraculously slackened to normal. Aabir moved forward and came to a halt before the woman who had once preoccupied all his senses.

149

'Hello there,' and he bent to kiss her flushed cheeks, without lingering on her neck to soak in the fragrance of her hair. He couldn't remember what all the fuss was about; her hair smelt of nothing in particular.

'Hello,' said Victoria. 'I'm sorry if I'm keeping you from work. I did so want to see you so I had Kimaya call you.'

'She sent me a message, telling me to plant myself here, yes,' Aabir sat down, feeling Victoria's appraising gaze. It was a habit she hadn't rid herself of; that quick sweep of the eyes that drank in a strand of hair that lay too flat, trousers that were only a little creased towards the ankles, cuff links that weren't set at just the right angle. It had made Aabir even more fastidious than usual. Persnickety, grinned Aabir.

Victoria put her book away and took a sip of her tea. 'This isn't very good tea, you know.'

Aabir felt a trifle annoyed. It was just like her to be disgruntled. He had once been enamoured by how difficult it was to please her, but the truth is, she was simply easily displeased.

'If you'd waited for me, I would have suggested the Viennese coffee,' he said, lightly. 'And the stuffed croissant. I love the stuffed croissant here. It can be messy but I've learnt to discipline it.'

He cocked his eye at his regular waiter; Aabir frequented Flurys enough to have a regular waiter. There were advantages to having a regular waiter at a place like Flurys; one actually got to place one's order within five minutes of one's arrival and thereafter was not kept waiting more than ten minutes for the dish to arrive. Aabir had no idea how the non-regulars dealt with the pace of the service. Obese tortoises moved faster than the waiters at Flurys.

Aabir placed his order and sat back to survey Victoria. She was always perfectly dressed, he had to admit. Clothes had never fallen as effortlessly on a human body as it did on Victoria Young.

'Allow me to apologize for my appalling behaviour that afternoon. I was caught off guard.'

'Of course you were,' murmured Victoria. 'I don't blame you one bit. I was startled myself.'

'I hope you enjoyed dinner?'

Victoria's face lit up. 'You have a charming place, Abe.' Aabir smiled; he hadn't that name in a while. 'Those waiters in coat-tails are a hoot. And that chocolate mousse...*heavenly*. I do think it's the only place in the city that Pa would have loved.'

She broke off uncertainly. Aabir skimmed over an uncomfortable silence lightly; he couldn't give a crow's claw about what Victoria's Pa would have loved. Victoria's Pa could stuff his face down his half-Windsor cravat.

'So, good old Cal has been less than welcoming?'

'I don't see how welcoming it can be really, if it's going to sport such beastly weather. I keep *sweating*!'

'I know, it's very inconvenient,' said Aabir, pushing the croissant towards her. 'Here, have some. Delicious.'

Victoria shook her head. 'Do you miss London, Aabir?'

'I do. I miss leaping out of bed on Saturday mornings to beat the crowds to Cornmarket.'

'You never leapt and you certainly never beat the crowds!'

Aabir chuckled. 'But that didn't stop me from fighting my way to the bread. That bread that smelt so divine and...'

'And then we'd tear off bits of it as we walked down the street. *Every* Saturday, Aabir!'

'We're suckers for tradition, apparently. What do you do with your Saturdays now?'

'I try to immerse myself in work.'

'Work?' Aabir was amused. 'A regular job?' He'd never pinned Victoria to be the kind to hold down a nine-to-five. She'd never professed an affinity for that sort of life and Aabir had imagined that she was the sort of woman who'd make a wealthy man very happy. And since Aabir had never had to work a part-time job to be able to afford life in England, the way so many of his friends had had to do, he'd made the mistake of imagining a wealthy life with Victoria by his side.

'I work at the art gallery down the road. It's a small place, but we have some awfully nice paintings. I meet some very interesting people.'

'Oh.'

'And I'm writing a book. That's what I spend my Saturdays doing.'

'Fiction?'

Victoria blushed. 'Historical romance.'

'Well, that's right up your alley then!'

'I know. I found an agent who liked the first couple of chapters and the proposal I'd drafted out. So I suppose I really should finish this project.'

'Certainly you should! I imagine your historical romances will just disappear off the shelves!'

'That's why I'm revisiting this Georgette Heyer,' Victoria gave *The Masqueraders* a nudge. 'For inspiration. Kimaya has an entire shelf of them.'

'Small world, isn't it?' said Aabir, more to himself than out loud.

'Really is. When she invited me to visit her and help her set up her shop, I didn't dream she'd be acquainted with you. Though I did…I did hope…I did wonder if I'd run into you.'

Aabir couldn't tear himself away from those eyes. They were a different pair of eyes from the ones he remembered. Sapphire dazzled his memory, while in reality he was gazing at steel; a steel that had seen a little more of the world than the smouldering sapphire had been willing to. He looked for the smile that he knew to be hovering on her lips, eager to break into a laugh, but it was gone, as though swallowed forever by the imperceptible wrinkle forming in the corner of her mouth. He caught her hand impulsively and she didn't draw away.

'Victoria,' he said, slowly, 'I sense a…' he searched for a word that would not hurt her, 'an ennui that I don't remember you ever possessing. Are you working too hard?'

Victoria drew her hand away. 'That wasn't the response I was looking for.'

Aabir watched her fingers fidget with the long-cold cup of tea. He imagined his grandmother's emerald ring on her finger, the heirloom that had been passed on from bride to bride through the generations, since Lord Hardinge had bestowed it on his great-grandfather. It struck him now that it would have been an imperfect fit.

'I hope you're happy, Vic.'

Victoria looked at him. Aabir Mookerjee had been the only person she had known who had never addressed her by that common abbreviation. She drew a sigh and leaned back against the chair, catching the eye of a young man whose pretence of reading a magazine was laughable. He flushed and tore his gaze away while Aabir held hers firmly.

'Of course.'

Aabir leaned in to deftly slice away a wedge of croissant without spilling any stuffing.

'Are you happy with your aristocratic suitors these days?'

Victoria thought of the pasty-faced Hon. Edmund, not yet the Earl of Elgin, and the well-meaning but oh-so clumsy Lord James, and shuddered a little.

'They're fine gentlemen,' she said. 'Very diverting.'

Aabir nodded. 'I'm glad you're in the company of fine, diverting young gents,' he said, emphatically.

Victoria bit her lip and suddenly stood up.

'I think I should leave,' she said, abruptly. 'I think I've kept Kimaya's chauffeur far too long.'

Aabir, a little taken aback, signalled for the bill. By the time he'd taken out his wallet, Victoria was stalking towards the door.

'Vic! Wait!'

He followed her in a hurry, but his progress was impeded as she spun around to face him.

'Oh, stop calling me that!'

Aabir stopped in his tracks, startled.

'I'm your young Victoria,' she whispered, in an undertone that he almost missed. He was unprepared for the waft of Fleurissimo that enveloped him, transporting him to a musty, second-hand bookshop in Sussex, unprepared for the kiss that dulled the chatter of the tea shop to a hum, unprepared for the anti-climax of the nothingness that he felt as she swept out the door, leaving him—the object of envy and disapproval.

But it was the look of affronted astonishment on Meenakshi Chatterjee's face that he was most unprepared for, as she gazed at him across a pink table and a chocolate rumball.

Chapter Sixteen

If there was one thing Thakuma did not have patience for, it was obtuseness, and Thakuma did not know anyone, living or dead, more obtuse than her daughter-in-law. She could be only thankful that her grandchildren had not inherited genes from *that* side of the family, but to watch her house be invaded by all sorts of riff-raff made Thakuma bristle. Even alive, Thakuma had not felt kindly towards the feeble-minded and as a spirit, her feelings towards them had not become any more charitable. Thakuma especially had little patience for youngsters who refused to heed the advice of the aged and the wise, especially when their own intellect was sadly wanting. She had often made it clear to her daughter-in-law that the purohit was not to be trusted and while Thakuma had walked the corridors of Mookerjee House, the man had been allowed to take fewer liberties. Since her death, Thakuma observed, the man had been running podgily amuck and had even managed to introduce one of his untrustworthy cronies into the house. If Aritra's wife had had the intuition to spot a bad egg when she saw one or the common sense to heed good advice, she would never have let some random girl enter her house. True, while the odd-job boy had frequently bungled up a chore, a few stern words and deprivation of sweets would have greatly improved his service. But Thakuma knew that Narayan and Purohitmoshai were in cahoots and something was fishy. Very fishy. Thakuma adjusted her lorgnette firmly. The house would need watching.

If Debjani Mookerjee had been aware that she had incurred the wrath of a terrorizing spirit, undoubtedly she would have been less cheerful while showing Geeta around the house. She didn't know that she was making her work a good deal easier by showing the young thief around. She did impress upon the fact that Thakuma's room was never to be entered, except in the morning to be aired and dusted and then locked again. Geeta looked at the antique chest of drawers and large mahogany closet, and wondered if the ring that her father had asked her to look for could be in there. She had been told that the old woman still kept a watch on the house from the coconut tree and she did not enjoy the prospect of rummaging around at night.

Mrs Mookerjee's own room was more inviting. Floral curtains fluttered at the window and the doors of the elaborate wardrobe, Geeta noticed, were hanging open.

'I want all the laundry to be well ironed and put away neatly on the shelves,' Mrs Mookerjee was saying, sternly. 'The boy before you used to be very haphazard about the way he folded my clothes.'

'Yes, Boudi,' said Geeta, meekly.

Mrs Mookerjee approved of this girl. She had none of the odd-job boy's cheek and neither did she grin like an idiot. She seemed like someone who would go about her work quietly. Mrs Mookerjee made up her mind to tell Mukul to be friendly towards her and put her at ease. Azim could be rough with newcomers sometimes.

Mukul, however, was not inclined to be friendly with the girl. He resented the fact that his friend, the odd-job boy, had been asked to leave and he wasn't going to go to any lengths to make his replacement comfortable if he could help it. Besides, her brother Babloo was often mean to him when he went to buy sweets from their shop and said cruel things about Mukul's protruding front teeth. Geeta was thus left to her own devices on her first day, in the company of Azim, the surly cook. Thakuma noted with approval that Azim did not take kindly to the girl's presence in his kitchen. For the first time Thakuma began to warm up to the man. Perhaps he wasn't such a bad sort after all.

158

'How long have you been working here?' asked Geeta, nibbling on an apple.

'A long time.'

'Do you like these people?'

'If I didn't, I wouldn't be working here.'

'I heard the neighbours would pay you more to go work there.'

Azim shrugged.

'Why won't you work there for more money?' persisted Geeta.

'None of your business.'

Thakuma smirked, but Geeta was not offended.

'It's a nice house,' said Geeta, looking out into the garden. 'I'm glad to get away from mine.'

Azim said nothing until curiosity got the better of him.

'Why?' he asked, not turning around from his task of mixing the chicken marinade.

It was Geeta's turn to shrug. Azim turned his head at her silence and cocked an eyebrow.

'None of your business,' said Geeta, grinning cheekily.

Azim scowled and turned away, and there was no drawing him out after that. With a toss of her braid, Geeta skipped out of the kitchen and crept up the stairs. She knew there were dogs lurking in the house, but Geeta was not afraid of dogs. Dogs, in fact, took to Geeta immediately, and Churchill, standing at the top of the stairs, allowed Geeta to enter his master's study without so much as a growl. Geeta even bent to ruffle his head a little. He was a doll. Not at all like the monster Boudi had made him out to be.

Geeta looked around at all the books in awe; this must be a man who studied a lot. How clever he must be. Geeta picked up the heavy fountain pen lying on Aabir's writing table and weighed it in her hand. She had never seen a pen so thick and heavy. These people must be very rich. No wonder her father wanted her to take that green ring. He had said that they had stolen it from someone and the police wanted her to steal it back for them. And if she managed to steal that ring, the police would give her father a lot of money and then perhaps she, Geeta, could also buy a heavy pen like this and learn to write beautifully with it. Her eyes caught sight of the gold paper-clips on the desk and she slipped some in her pocket without thinking, before creeping out of the room again. Thakuma shook a leaf threateningly.

Chapter Seventeen

Aabir Mookerjee was not pleased to see his oldest friend. Indeed, it may be noticed that Aabir Mookerjee was seldom pleased to see his oldest friend.

'What?' he said, curtly.

In the background of the Calcutta Club reading room, Sabir hovered apologetically. When Aabir had excitedly discovered a hidden recipe book in the recesses of the disarranged bookshelves, he had informed Sabir that he was to let no one talk to him. Sometimes Aabir forgot that his favourite bearer was not his personal butler and there were some tasks that were undoable. Not that Sabir hadn't tried to keep Rana Raina from bursting in on Mookerjee saab, but when Rana Raina had made up his mind to burst in on someone, burst in he must.

'Don't you ever get tired of looking at food?'

'I was contemplating the strawberry pandowdy as part of the E&B repertoire and I was in the middle of taking down the recipe, when you interrupted me with your utter uselessness.'

'I don't know what women see in you. I just don't,' said

Rana Raina, shaking his head and sinking into the sofa beside Aabir.

'Allow me to reciprocate the sentiment.'

'Oh please. Bitches love me. Why wouldn't they?'

'Firstly, you're insufferable. Secondly, you're adulterous. Thirdly, you...'

'Hey, *hey*!' Rana Raina sat up with a frown.

'What? *What*?'

'I haven't been adulterous for a whole two months now. This Mia babe man, she's driving me nuts.'

'Mia? Who's Mia? You haven't told me about any Mia!'

'Meenakshi. Freakin. Chatterjee. Why can't you ever remember?'

'Oh. Her. Right.'

'She's driving me up the wall. She just won't give *in*. Do you know we spent the last weekend at Vedic Village?'

'You checked her into a spa hotel already?'

'I checked *us* in. And she sashayed around in a white bikini all day and then just fell asleep on my bed in a black négligée. I just wanted to...'

'Spare me the details.'

'Oh, of course. Because you've been living it up all over town in the arms of some blonde, huh?'

Aabir's surprise wiped the sardonic disregard off his face. Rana Raina hooted with laughter. 'I know everything my friend. I watch you all the time. I. Am. Those giant spectacles in *The Great Gatsby*.'

'Dr T.J. Eckleburg, you ignoramus.'

'Stop changing the topic.'

'And you're no Eckleburg. Mia Chatterjee let you in on

this little piece of gossip, didn't she?'

Rana Raina looked deflated. 'She may have. She was all in a huff about it. Something about how you've always blown her off for coffee, but as soon as some bit of white trash comes along…'

'We're talking about Victoria Young,' said Aabir, sharply.

Rana Raina sat up a little more, his jaw hanging open in a manner that would have made a passing stranger regard him with the kind of sympathy that one reserves for the feeble-minded.

'Victoria Young?'

'Yes.'

'*The* Victoria Young?'

'I believe so.'

'Victoria Young of the The Past?'

'The same.'

'What…what is she doing here?'

'Turns out she's a friend of Kimaya's and came to visit.'

'Kimaya? Who's Kimaya? Why are there suddenly so many women in your life?'

'Of The Mad Hatter,' said Aabir, dispassionately.

'Oh. Her. The hot baker. Boy! Small world!'

'I agree.'

'Tiny world.'

'Yes, you've hit the miniscule nail on the head.'

'So, now what?'

Aabir looked quizzical. 'What do you mean?'

'What are you going to do?'

'Nothing.'

'Nothing!'

'Nothing.'

'But! It's Victoria! You've been kissing her in tea shops. You must put her in a red saree and marry her immediately. I'll send the pompous father a photograph and my heartiest congratulations.'

Aabir chuckled. 'The man will have a heart attack over his suckling pig.'

'Aabir, that was your father.'

Aabir looked sober. 'Oh, you're right.'

'So you've been kissing her with no plans to marry her?' asked Rana Raina, who seemed to be in need of some clarification. He stood up and thumped Aabir's back. 'Good for you, man. My job here is done.'

'It's not what you think it is.'

'It never is,' smirked Rana Raina.

'Oh bugger off and find some luck with that Mia woman, will you? Before the whole blooming club is aflame with the story.'

'That's true. No club takes to gossip the way Cal Club does. I'm happy to try some damage control. I wonder why she likes you. You just stop short of being rude to her.'

'Some women like that,' said Aabir, returning to his well-thumbed cookbook.

Rana Raina pursed his lips. 'I'll have her. Just you watch.'

'I'd rather not, really.'

'Anyway. I have parties to be at. Let's meet Victoria over some dinner and feed her some *chicken jalfrezi*,' chortled Rana Raina.

'You just want her to spout tears like she did over those tandoori chicken chops in that time you visited me, don't you?'

'Don't remind me! I was *not* expecting delicious Indian food in Belgravia! And what was with her? Tandoori chicken, man! It's not even spicy!'

Rana Raina left the library, sniggering. Aabir looked at the recipe and bit his lip. Something like an old-fashioned strawberry pandowdy could make or break the E&B menu.

෴

There were a great many things wrong about Geeta, as anyone who cared to have a discussion with Thakuma on the subject, on a sultry afternoon, would have discovered. But no one did and Thakuma was left to fulminate against the girl, by herself, atop the tree. Yet, even Thakuma could not deny that what the girl did not lack was nerve. The kind of nerve that one will notice in dogs who dig up flower beds in order to conceal a beloved bone, even though it means a dreadful walloping and perhaps a night in the kennel for it.

Just the other afternoon, when Debjani Mookerjee had fallen asleep in front of the television in her room, Geeta had crept inside and turned the wardrobe key oh-so-silently. Thakuma had watched in outrage as she had rummaged about, quiet as a mime artist, evidently looking for something. Thakuma wanted to know just what it was that she was looking for. Money? Jewellery? Didn't she know that valuables were locked up in banks?

Evidently, her hunt had yielded no results, for she had snuck out of the room empty-handed. There was no one to accost her in the hall, but had there been, Thakuma was sure that the girl would have had an excuse ready at the tip of her tongue. Servants these days had taken to all measures of insubordination. Thakuma remembered an age when the mere sound of her father's shoes would send the footmen in a tizzy. Not that her father had been oppressive. Once a maid—a young girl of ten—had taken an ivory bangle from her mother's dressing table, but was later discovered by young Tusharbala, who had frog-marched her to her father. Thakuma's father had removed his spectacles, looked down at the cowering little girl and asked her gently—'Why did you take it?'

'It was pretty,' she replied in a faltering whisper.

'Then you should come to me when you want something and not take it from another person's room.'

The little girl had wept, more out of surprise than fear. Tusharbala had later watched in amazement as the girl was rewarded, instead of punished, with a small ivory bangle. 'Kindness will find you friends who will stay when you need them, Bala,' her father had said, fondling her head.

Thakuma wondered whether she had been able to follow her father's advice. Most people would not describe Thakuma as being *kind*, but many had been surprised by her moments of unexpected compassion. Mukul, for instance, had remained a terrified yet devoted ally of Thakuma. When Aabir and he had both contracted jaundice at the same time, Thakuma, ignoring all Mrs Mookerjee's protestations, had had another bed made up in Aabir's room and had tended to him with as much care as she did her own grandson. Mukul's father had cried with gratitude, but Thakuma had brusquely waved him away, telling him to contaminate some other room with his tears.

Geeta, however, was unaware that Thakuma could be compassionate. She had only heard tales of autocracy, and had anyone told her that she could appeal to Thakuma's kinder side, she would not have believed them. When she dusted Thakuma's room every morning, she tried to jiggle the locks with her hairpins, but nothing worked. Once the grandfather clock had chimed outside, just as she had stuck her hairpin into the chest of drawers, and she had leapt up with a cry. She hated that ugly old monstrosity in the hallway; it always seemed to leer at her and sing at odd hours. Mukul had told her that Thakuma's ghost probably lurked in there on rainy nights and since then Geeta had hurried past the giant clock without looking at it.

Thakuma decided that if the living inhabitants of the house were going to be oblivious to the goings on, then it was the responsibility of the undead to restore law and order. In Thakuma's experience, with the appropriate sort of influence, the youth were as easily led astray as they were led down the path of virtue. There was no saving the wretched adult set in his wicked ways, but a young girl who has known no better can certainly be rescued from the dredges of a dishonest life.

Not very many people could be depended upon to not be scared witless at the sight of an austere old lady descending down a coconut tree. Thakuma therefore chose her moment wisely and made her appearance only when Azim had stepped out into the kitchen garden to inspect the pumpkin patch. If he was surprised to see Thakuma looking deceptively comfortable on a pumpkin, like a trapeze artist who has practised her balancing act well, he did not bat an eyelid. He regarded her, instead, in customary sullenness, assuming correctly, that she had descended from her coconut abode with good reason.

'Your skills have improved greatly since my death, Azim.'

Azim grunted.

'I know for a fact that Aatreyeedi crept downstairs in the middle of the night to have more of the carrot cake you had made last week.'

'And still you will not let me have the posto-bora recipe,' growled Azim. It was evident that he was not about to forgive Thakuma for having denied him the knowledge that made the poppy-seed kababs so irresistible to the members of Mookerjee House.

Thakuma looked at him sternly through her lorgnette.

'Azim, you have allowed a dishonest person to infiltrate your kitchen.'

'She has nothing to do in my kitchen and therefore is none of my business,' replied Azim, curtly.

'But you know that she is dishonest?'

'It's none of my business,' insisted the surly cook.

'Don't be ungrateful, Azim. You know you're not taking up the Bajorias on their offer because you'll lose all the autonomy that you have here. And you can threaten Boudi all you want, but I can see right through you.'

Azim scowled. There was no getting rid of the woman even after she had left this world; it was most unfair.

'This girl, Geeta. Do you know that she feeds the dogs across the road?'

This bit of trivia did not excite Azim. 'She likes dogs. Dogs like her.' What was Thakuma getting at?

'When a dog likes a human being, Azim, you can be assured that there is good in her. Even though it may be so far concealed, it is hidden to the human eye.'

Azim snorted. 'A neighbour of mine once stabbed his wife

to death and the dogs on the street were devoted to him.'

'Something tells me they weren't devoted to the wife,' said Thakuma, archly.

Azim said nothing.

'You do not steal, Azim.'

Azim looked insulted. 'Of course not.'

'And you rarely lie.'

'I *never* lie!'

'Now, now, Azim. Last month you claimed you had to visit your brother when actually you were gambling at a card tournament.'

Azim flushed. Losing money at the card tournament still rankled.

'Let the girl notice these things about you.'

Azim was confused. What good will that do?

'Just do it, Azim. And if all works out, you may be whipping up all the posto-bora that you want very soon.'

Azim frowned. Thakuma had often had strange ideas and they had evidently become stranger still after her demise. But he knew a raise would be inevitable if he got the posto-bora just right and a raise is exactly what he needed to recover the loss incurred at that ridiculous tournament.

Chapter Eighteen

The odd-job boy was whistling for the first time in days. He had just discovered the all-consuming joy of stirring smooth cream into sugar and eggs. He had noted Vishnu's jealousy with unholy pleasure as Kimaya almost wept with happiness when he grilled the crème brûlée to perfection. The odd-job boy couldn't help thinking that Aabirda was a stand-up fellow. Not many men would have put themselves to the trouble of looking for another job for some stripling who had been fired by his mother for bringing home the wrong cake. The odd-job boy didn't know much about foreign desserts. Pastries, pies and puddings were all the same to him. But he was fast discovering that making them was a piece of cake and he was happy to be of service to Aabirda's friend, who seemed to own some sort of restaurant which served all these nameless sweetmeats.

Aabirda's friend had spent a fruitful day in the kitchens of The Mad Hatter. She untied her apron as she sank into the couch, her face flushed from culinary exertions. She touched the chocolate stains that ran across the words—*There's much a-dough about muffin*—and was vexed by the inconvenient manner in which her heart sank a little. Pepper, who had managed to cajole a mouthful of custard from the odd-job boy's fingers, looked up hopefully at her mistress.

'Do you want to be a fat dog?' asked Kimaya, sternly.

Pepper's fervent panting implied that indeed she did not mind being a fat dog. In fact, Pepper saw no reason why she should not be a fat dog at the cost of regular helpings of custard.

'I see the crème brûlée has conquered yet another heart. Have you seen Victoria?'

Pepper looked mournfully at the guest bedroom that had remained impenetrable all morning. Pepper had whined. Pepper had clawed. The door had remained shut. If there was one thing that Pepper disliked more than afternoon siestas, it was a locked door. Pepper was never more offended than she was when faced with a locked door.

Kimaya sighed. Victoria had returned from Flurys in a curious mood. She had answered Tanuja in monosyllables, disappointed Vishnu by picking at his signature chicken curry and made Pepper quite miserable by refusing to tickle her ears. There had been no word from Aabir either, other than a friendly message to say that his sister had devoured half the cake—a clear sign that she had enjoyed it. 'I see you're making yourself quite indispensable,' he had said, and she wondered if she should read more into the sentence like women were likely to do.

Kimaya heard the bedroom door open followed by the sound of light footsteps. Pepper scrambled to her feet, forgiving of the locked door already.

'Pepper.' There was something in Kimaya's voice that made

her stand still; a Cocker recognized a forbidding tone when she heard one.

Kimaya didn't look up from the Facebook browser open on her iPad when Victoria entered the room softly. She pretended to not notice that even with tousled hair and in a polka-dotted baby-doll nightdress she looked plenty desirable. Kimaya suddenly resented having hips too wide and arms too thick. Of course Aabir was going to fall in love all over again; a man would be crazy to not be drawn to the effortless beauty of Victoria Young, to resist that easy grace and spontaneous elegance that most women spent their lives trying to achieve. Kimaya felt her heart sink again, and this time she was less vexed about it. Funny, old Aabir Mookerjee had begun to grow on her. Persnickety Aabir. Stodgy Aabir. But all in all, an adorable Aabir, who, much like crème brûlée, liked to conceal the cream under a crusty surface.

171

'Kimaya.'

Kimaya looked up from her iPad. 'Oh, hello. You've emerged at last. Slept well?' Kimaya sounded far too exuberant even to her own ears.

'Er...yes...' Victoria looked doubtful. 'Do you still have any of that watermelon juice?'

Kimaya, who would normally have sprung to the aid of her guest, pointed towards the kitchen. 'Vishnu is your man.'

She watched Victoria disappear in search of watermelon juice and return with a glass of the cool, pink beverage. Victoria sank into an armchair and signalled to Pepper to join her. The dog bounded over in a moment, tail all a-wag.

'She missed you,' said Kimaya, gruffly. 'How was Flurys? Did you try any of the cakes?'

'No, but Aabir ordered a stuffed croissant that he seemed to enjoy.'

'I imagine him slicing it into neat little portions with a knife and fork, as opposed to just taking a massive bite out of it,' said Kimaya, absently, wondering if she should upload a photograph of the latest batch of crème brûlée to The Mad Hatter Facebook page.

'That's exactly what he did, yes,' said Victoria, looking a little surprised. She patted Pepper absently. 'What had we planned to do today?'

'Drinks at the Taj. You'll like it. I have a saree that you can wear with that black lace crop-top.'

'I'm going to fall flat on my face. Sarees look awfully complicated.'

'One gets used to it. I remember having to dance in a saree for school cultural evenings. I did almost fall flat on my face this one time.' Kimaya looked up to find a smile hovering on Victoria's lips. 'Do you want to invite Aabir?' she asked abruptly

The smile disappeared. 'For drinks? No, I don't think that's a good idea.'

'Oh, I thought you two might want to catch up on good times, you know.'

'We did, at Fur Elise.'

And was he happy to see you? Did your eyes bring back memories? Did your smile make his heart skip a beat like it used to? Kimaya bit her tongue. 'It's Flurys. Which is not the same as the piece by Beethoven.'

'Flurys,' repeated Victoria. She unfolded her feet from under her legs and stood up. She set her glass of juice down on the coaster and pulled out the piano stool.

'Aabir and I used to play a duet sometimes,' she said. Kimaya watched as she opened the lid of the upright piano that was set against the wall, under a grand framed photograph of Aman and Kimaya on the evening of their engagement. Victoria contemplated it for a moment.

'You look beautiful,' she said, finally. 'Indian women really are beautiful. Sometimes I wish I was, you know.'

'Wish you were beautiful?' asked, Kimaya, aghast.

'In the dark haired, flashing eyes, swivelling hips way. This entire blonde-haired, blue-eyed business is such a cliché.'

Kimaya started to laugh.

'What?' asked Victoria, defensively.

'Whoever said that grass is always greener on the other side really hit the nail on the head.'

Victoria shrugged and turned towards the piano. She stared at the keys for a moment. Pepper had cocked up her ears, already on eager tenterhooks.

'He was no maestro,' said Victoria, 'but I was only an average pianist.' Her fingers moved softly over the keys. 'We used to play this all the time, though.'

Kimaya did not recognize Beethoven's Spring Sonata, but she did recognize melancholic nostalgia. She watched Victoria's fingers fly deftly over the black-and-white keys that Kimaya herself had not touched since her husband had died. She watched Victoria's reflection in the window—the eyes that were fixed upon the framed photograph, the mouth that was imperceptible until it quivered only a little. Kimaya padded out of the room softly, leaving Pepper to witness the tears that never welled over and the music that never stumbled, not once, even though it had not been played in two years.

&

'Pudding shots.'

'No pudding shots, sir.'

Aabir Mookerjee glared at the man in the ridiculous top hat and leaned in surreptitiously. The waiter backed away, a little alarmed.

'I'm telling you, they're not on the menu yet, but there'll be some in the kitchen. Mrs Kapoor told me to come in and sample some.'

'No, sir.'

Aabir drew in a long breath. 'Listen to me.'

'Yes, sir.'

174   'I've been told to get started on the chocolate pudding shots. Mrs Kapoor is going to join me soon.'

'Yes, sir.'

'Good, chocolate pudding shots then. Just one.'

'No pudding shots, sir.'

If Aabir Mookerjee was the type to gnash his teeth, he would have done just that. Instead, he closed his eyes and pondered on happier things. Things, like the substantially higher intelligence quotients of the waiters at E&B. He wondered if it was The Mad Hatter policy to hire half-wits in order to drive customers quite mad.

'There is chocolate pudding, sir.'

'Pudding *shots*. Chocolate pudding *shots*!'

'No pudding shots, sir.'

A strangled cry escaped Aabir's lips and the group of teenagers behind him, who were clearly skipping college on a Wednesday afternoon, giggled.

'Aabir! I'm sorry, I'm late! Hiren, tell Chef to bring out the pudding shots, will you?'

'Yes, madam.'

Aabir sputtered as Kimaya drew up a chair.

'God, it's hot outside!' she said, pushing her sunglasses on her head.

'That waiter is an obtuse and asinine imbecile!'

'Language, Mookerjee!'

'I've been demanding pudding shots for ten minutes now!'

'Maybe if you'd asked nicely…'

'I did ask nicely!' hooted Aabir. 'Don't you sit there and accuse me of not being nice to your oafs!'

Kimaya giggled. 'Calm down. You're terrifying those kids.'

'They should be in class. And allow me to say that your sunglasses are hurting my eyes.'

'What do you mean?'

'They are larger than your face.'

'They're supposed to be.'

'And they're *yellow*.'

'Yup.'

'Who wears *yellow* sunglasses?'

'Gwen Stefani. January Jones.'

'I'd suggest…'

'And Lady Gaga has a pair very similar to this one!' Kimaya brought her sunglasses down to her eyes again, with a flourish. Aabir balked.

'I am not at all surprised that Gaga is the style you would choose. Not one bit surprised.'

'Stodge,' said Kimaya, removing her sunglasses.

'Where have you fine ladies been gadding about all day?'

'I dragged Vic to New Market to buy some supplies for Mad Hatter.'

Aabir grinned. 'Oh Lord!'

It struck Kimaya that he shed about five years when he smiled like that. The laugh lines around his eyes were just right.

'She did not enjoy herself,' she admitted, deciding that Aabir didn't need to know about the violinless duet that had been performed that morning.

'No, I can't imagine her enjoying that. If there's anything Victoria hates, it's grime. And New Market, in spite of its infinite possibilities, leaves much to be desired in the sanitation department.'

Kimaya giggled. 'Beggars accosted her and tangled their fingers in her hair.'

'Oh dear. Oh no.'

'The smell from the pig market almost made her throw up.'

'Oh, the pig market! That doesn't even bother me anymore.'

'Me neither! I didn't even realize there was a pig-stench until Vic said she was going to bring up her lunch.'

'And of course she had her first sight of a man treating the world as his personal toilet.'

Aabir doubled up in laughter. 'You're horrible. You *knew* she was going to hate it!'

'Me? Of course not. She said she wanted to help with all things Hatter, so I took her out for my weekly jaunt to New Market.'

Aabir looked disbelievingly at Kimaya, who returned his gaze with a wide-eyed innocence that Aabir rightly concluded was a mere performance.

'She's upstairs taking a nap, now. We're going to Taj for cocktails and dinner tonight.'

'That's much more her thing. Poor Victoria. She'd never be able to survive the third world.'

'Good thing then, that you had to call it all off,' said Kimaya, in simulated nonchalance.

'Pudding shots, madam.'

Kimaya glared at the waiter. Aabir was right. The man really was an obtuse and asinine imbecile. All afternoon Kimaya had struggled with the urge to call Aabir on a pretext…any pretext…and find out if love, like the irrepressible red ixora in summer, had bloomed again. Victoria had remained silent as a tomb on the subject and Kimaya had never been one to handle suspense well. And just when she thought she had got her toe into the subject, this man appeared with pudding shots. There was nothing like chocolate to distract Aabir from the topic at hand. Kimaya had had to invent a whole new tempting dessert to lure him away from his own kitchens.

'Yes, entirely a good thing. Sometimes one needs a little distance to gain perspective. Good God, Kimaya. What *are* these things?'

Kimaya stared at Aabir as his spoon hovered over the tiny brownie-encased molten chocolate pudding. Had he just admitted a preference for a Victorialess existence? Did he no longer care to revisit his great catastrophic romance?

'No, I don't think this should be demolished by a spoon,' Aabir was saying. Kimaya watched as he put an oval brownie into his mouth and smiled as his eyes lit up when the warm molten pudding inside oozed into his mouth in a burst of chocolate, Kahlua and cream.

When Aabir opened his eyes and drank in the top-hatted waiters milling around, the stools that looked like tree stumps and the fictitious woodland that he was in, it struck him that The Mad Hatter had become the stuff that childhood dreams were made of.

'Kimaya,' he said, slowly. 'I admit defeat.'

'What?'

'I'm beaten. The E&B mousse simply does not compare.'

'Oh, that's not true. Do you know who helped me bake it?'

'Surely not Victoria! Once she tried her hand at muffins and it turned out to be a mess because she'd mistaken semolina for flour!'

Kimaya choked. 'No, not Victoria. That little odd-job boy you sent my way. Turns out he has a talent for baking!'

Aabir looked far from jubilant. 'All these months he sat in my house burning my mother's clothes and mixing up cake orders, and he comes to you and transforms into a regular Vianne Rocher?'

'The fault, dear Persnickety, is not in our stars, but in ourselves.'

Aabir scowled. 'I never did like Cassius.'

'I liked Brutus even less.'

'Listen to me. Stop beating around the bush. If you don't agree to have Mad Hatter cater the dessert section in E&B, I'm going to have to burn this place down, do you understand?'

Kimaya's eyes lit up. 'That's a wonderful idea!'

'Great. I'm going to have my lawyer draft an agreement immediately.'

Aabir leapt to his feet and before Kimaya knew it, he had brushed his lips against her cheek and shot out the door. She blushed and looked up to find the odd-job boy's grinning face flattened against the round glass pane of the kitchen door. A thumbs-up indicated to him that the brownie shots that he had helped bake that afternoon had been a resounding success.

Chapter Nineteen

Thakuma loathed people who found the need to rest their feet on the centre table in the living room. She loathed people who dribbled tea down their front because they were too slovenly to care. And she especially loathed people who ingratiated themselves with others only to serve their own selfish ends.

Had Purohitmoshai known that he was being subject to such wrathful scrutiny, he may have removed his hefty ankles from the delicate centre table and dabbed at the tea that he had spilt on his kurta, but he could have not stopped himself from delivering the news that he had come to deliver.

'I have come to remove all your miseries, Mrs Mookerjee.'

'Nothing can remove my miseries,' moaned Mrs Mookerjee, who was inclined to be overdramatic for the purohit since he was the only one who paid any heed to her. Her children had long ago stopped taking her theatrics seriously and her husband had never even feigned interest. Sometimes she felt that The Holy One was her only friend. 'My son is destined to be a bachelor. Today I tried to ask him if there is a girl he can see himself settling down with, and he walked out of the room.'

'I know of a girl. She is perfect for your son. *Perfect.*'

Mrs Mookerjee put down the orange cream biscuit. 'Who is she? What does she do? Is she pretty?'

'She has just returned from Glasgow after finishing her Masters in Law. Her mother wants her to be married before she finds herself a job.'

Mrs Mookerjee nodded her approval.

'She is one of the most graceful and competent girls I have ever seen. She can make an Indian fish curry as well as she can make...what was it she made the other day... er... something Italian...a delicious pasta something or the other... very tasty, Mrs Mookerjee! I never thought that those tasteless strips of flour can be so tasty!'

'Perfect!'

'And I have seen her very involved in all family occasions. She is very homely, this girl, and yet has a promising career.'

'When can we meet her?'

'I will set up a meeting as soon as I can. I don't know whether she wants to get married just now. She was arguing with her mother that...'

'I don't understand this generation! When I was young, we all wanted to be married and have children. The ambitious ones wanted to teach, but not at the cost of being single all their lives. Nowadays being married is like a shameful thing!'

'I have told her that Aabir is a gentleman and boys like him do not come around every day. Any day now he will be taken and then she would have lost her chance.'

'You are my true well-wisher, Purohitmoshai!'

'Yes, Mrs Mookerjee, I am. I know that you have promised me an expensive gift, but it is because I love you like I would have my own daughter that I go to such lengths for you.'

'Yes, you will be repaid if Aabir can be convinced to marry this girl. Your gift is very expensive and very big. And you know...it's been in the family for years.'

'I think I've heard Thakuma talk about it,' said The Holy One, his eyes gleaming.

'Yes, she was very fond of it. That is why I can't give it away to just anyone!'

'I will not fail you, Debjani,' said Purohitmoshai, tears of gratitude in his eyes. He noticed Geeta dusting the cabinet on the other side of the room, but did not think that the conversation would interest her enough to relay it to her father. What he did not know was that it interested her enough to relay it to her brother.

'Purohitmoshai is helping Mrs Mookerjee look for a wife for her son,' she giggled, when she went to buy sweet curd from her father's shop in the evening.

Babloo frowned. 'Yes, he was doing that, but now he's stopped.'

'You don't know anything. He came this afternoon only with news of some girl and Mrs Mookerjee was very happy. When are you going to be married?'

'Don't ask stupid questions,' growled Babloo, and pushed her out of the shop.

Geeta didn't know why her brother was always so rough. And her father had not even come out to see her. Geeta decided she didn't miss her family. Not one bit. Everyone at Mookerjee House was so polite. Mukul didn't seem to like her very much and Aatreyeedi had not spoken a word to her, but Aabirda was always gentle and even Boudi was nice to her. Azim was very strict with her and would not even let her take a biscuit from Aabir's tin, even though she was sure that Aabir himself would not mind.

183

Geeta pondered the silent and efficient figure of Azim. The other evening, when writing his accounts for the day for Mrs Mookerjee, he had returned the four rupees that had been left over from the money that had been given to him to fetch groceries. Geeta had been astounded. She knew that even Mukul fibbed about the price of vegetables in the market so he could save to buy himself a movie ticket now and then.

'I'm sure Boudi will not mind if you keep the change,' she had said.

'If she wants me to have it, she will give it to me. But I will not keep it without her knowledge,' Azim had said, not lifting his eyes from the little notebook he was scribbling in.

Geeta had meant to ask him if he knew anything about the emerald, but she didn't. She had a feeling Azim would not appreciate her curiosity in the family affairs and even if he did know something, he would not share his information with her. She offered to chop the beans for him instead and was grateful that he let her. Later, she reflected that she was so much happier in her new house and that if she could put off the search for the stolen ring, she could spend more time here. She was beginning to find it difficult to believe that anyone in this house would have filched anything, and for the first time she wondered if her father had fabricated a story to remove her from her house for having stolen from her mother's cupboard. That made Geeta feel very small indeed.

Chapter Twenty

Aabir Mookerjee was not a vigorous swimmer. He liked to float in the clear aquamarine waters of the swimming pool, after most people had vacated it, and ruminate on the twists and turns of life or, if E&B had had a harrowing day, on a chicken a la kiev without butter. Other young men may smirk at this lean, brooding figure as they splash by with powerful breast strokes, but they would be mistaken in their assumption that Aabir Mookerjee was incapable of a robust butterfly or an energetic back stroke. As a child, Aabir had spent many a happy afternoon propelling himself with force from the diving board. However, with manhood had come the disinclination for physical exertion and the swimming pool had turned into a space for languid unwinding. Rana Raina, who spent his mornings perspiring over weights at the gymnasium, grumbled that Fate had dealt Aabir an unfair metabolism; no man who consumed butter and sugar at the rate at which Aabir Mookerjee did should be allowed to have a bulge-free stomach.

Aabir was in a good mood today and was even considering some gentle paddling. E&B and The Mad Hatter were going to be the culinary force in the city. People would be flocking around in herds soon. Aabir debated between offering crème brûlée on the all-night menu or the red velvet cheesecake. He would have to discuss this with Kimaya. Aabir himself preferred crème brûlée, but he often found that just when he was prepared to dislike a red velvet cheesecake, it surprised him. It was probably all that cream cheese.

Aabir couldn't wait to have the logistics of the merger all sorted. Unlike the average Calcuttan, Aabir Mookerjee liked to progress from the mere discussion of an idea over tea and sweetened biscuits; he liked to have it executed as soon as possible. It is uncommon for the average Calcuttan to be able to muster up anything other than flagless lethargy, and many a grand idea—the Bengalis are known to make up in intellect what they lack in diligence—have remained in that embryo stage a grand idea. The fact that Kimaya Kapoor was not a Bengali gave Aabir further reason to hope, without a twinge of guilt towards his Bengali brethren, that this partnership was not about to fail.

In fact, Kimaya was really quite a sport. That Aman chap must have been a man of good taste. Not that Kimaya had ever really discussed him at length, but Aabir was seldom wrong about these things. He wondered if she would ever consider being married to someone else. Aabir gazed up at the yellow lights that lit up the poolside and came to the conclusion that it would be a shame if she didn't. Attractive woman, Kimaya, in spite of her deplorable penchant for odd attire. Not once had he seen her without something ridiculous on her person. Moustached shoes…yellow sunglasses for God's sake. And yet she could be quite pleasing to the eye…definitely attractive.

Symmetry, decided Aabir, was the key to good looks. And Kimaya Kapoor was perfectly symmetrical. Her lips especially were symmetrically wide, so much so that the hint of a smile could light up her face. And her hands, bereft of any rings, he had noticed, were symmetrically delicate.

Aabir spluttered and floundered to his feet when a perfectly symmetrical pair of breasts, barely sheathed in a scarlet swimsuit, loomed above him.

'Aabir Mookerjee.'

Aabir groaned. It had been a good day and the last thing he wanted was for Mia Chatterjee to ruin his solitary swim.

'Hi. Hello. Hi,' he said, shaking some water out of his ears.

'I imagined you to be masterfully swimming across the pool,' smiled Meenakshi Chatterjee. It struck Aabir that the ghastly pink could not be the natural colour of her lips, which, Aabir observed with some satisfaction, was far from symmetrical.

187

'Now, why would you do that?'

The Calcutta Club pool was rarely inhabited by youngsters. Aabir couldn't help noticing that Mia Chatterjee's presence had garnered some attention amongst the old fogeys. Aabir groaned. Of course they were going to talk about her for days and how Aabir Mookerjee—you know, Aritra Mookerjee's son, who owns what'sitcalled…that restaurant next to Mocambo—was hobnobbing with her.

'Did you learn to swim as a child?'

'In the Tollygunge Club, yes. I mauled my trainer when he tried to throw me into the deep end.'

Miss Chatterjee threw her head back and laughed exuberantly. Heads turned and Aabir winced.

'Oh dear,' she said. 'That made my cap come loose. Do be a dear and fix it.'

She tugged her cap off and handed it to Aabir, shaking her wet hair loose.

'Er...' he said. Miss Chatterjee was standing very close to him now and a waft of heady perfume hit him as she did her hair up again.

'Come now. I always have the attendant help me with my cap. I never seem to get the seams right.'

'I haven't the foggiest idea how to use one of these things,' said Aabir. 'I suppose one just stretches it *so* and slides it on *so*.'

He looked at his work on Miss Chatterjee's head. The cap looked odd, but she seemed to be pleased.

'Why, thank you, Aabir.'

'Right. I'll be off then.'

'Oh, no. Already?'

'Yes. Er...I have a dinner engagement. Must rush.'

Mia Chatterjee looked disapppointed. 'I was hoping we could grab a bite. There's a special menu today in the dining hall.'

'I think I saw Rana Raina lurking around the bar. I'm sure he'll be up for a meal. He's entertaining too. Oh dear. I'm already so late. Must be off. I'll see you around.'

Aabir waded towards the steps and hauled himself out of the pool. Really, what did Rana Raina see in that woman? She wasn't even symmetrical.

Aabir didn't know what had compelled him to wear his charcoal grey waistcoat that day, but as he buttoned up in the changing room, it struck him that he was dressed for dinner and wondered if it would be terribly rude to drop in on the ladies on their night out. No, perhaps Victoria wouldn't like that. Aabir combed his hair carefully and surveyed himself. No, Victoria would *not* like that, but then it wasn't Victoria he wanted to see anyway.

❧

When she stepped through the glass doors and into the gleaming hallway of the Taj Bengal hotel, Victoria sighed. Here at last was a place free of dust, pollution and beggars. She could sit back and enjoy a cool martini and perhaps some roast duck; she had had enough of these Indian gravies and oily vegetables. She just wanted some crunchy rocket leaves with a sprinkling of blue cheese and *no* curd to 'cool the system'. If they went easy on the spices, they wouldn't need a saucer of curd anyway.

Victoria's saree got entangled between her legs and she kept having to clutch at Kimaya for support. Tanuja had draped it around her expertly and stuck it with many pins, promising that it would not come apart, but as Victoria minced forward now, she was not so sure.

'Don't think about it and it'll be fine,' said Kimaya, who was gliding forth as though she didn't have six yards of cloth precariously hanging on her body.

'We should have just worn dresses.'

'You wear dresses all the time, Vic. I think you should take that saree back with you. It looks so much better against your skin-tone. I don't know why I thought that shade of yellow would flatter me.'

'A couple of my friends did return from India with sarees, but I don't think they ever got around to wearing them.'

'YouTube has videos that'll show you how to wear a saree.'

'Kimaya. I just want a martini.'

'Almost there. Almost there.'

Kimaya led Victoria into the wood-panelled restaurant that overlooked the pool. A line of steel tureens had been laid out for the dinner buffet, coming to an end with an extravagant spread of dessert. Duck in Raspberry Sauce, read Victoria with relief. Grilled Fish with Salt and Vinegar Potatoes. Victoria's heart sang.

'Let's get that martini, shall we?' she said, cheerfully.

'Oooh. Vic,' said Kimaya, gazing out of the French windows at the lawn on the other side of the pool.

'What is it?'

'Have you ever wanted to crash a wedding?'

'What? Of course not! Don't be silly.'

'I think there's a first time for everything.'

'First time for what?' said a voice behind them.

Kimaya spun around while Victoria did a double take.

'Aabir!' squealed Kimaya. 'How dapper you look! What are you doing here?'

'I had half a mind of inviting myself for dinner, but I know it's frightfully rude, so I'll leave after my first drink. You have my word.'

'Don't be silly. Stay for dinner.'

Victoria compressed her lips.

'Look, we managed to get Vic into a saree.'

'So I see. How elegant,' said Aabir, turning towards his old flame. How she paled in contrast to this dazzling young woman in forest green. Kimaya was truly captivating when she had her hair pulled away from her shoulders like that and her blouse fell away from her neck, oh so bewitchingly.

Then, feeling rather uncharitable, Aabir remembered that few women could carry off a dress with the kind of finesse with which Victoria had worn a particularly revealing number once.

'I was proposing we gate-crash that wedding there,' said Kimaya. 'We're certainly dressed for it.'

Aabir looked appalled. 'You can't be serious!'

'What? It'll be so much fun. And I see some white folks. We'll blend in easily!'

'Hare-brained idea,' muttered Victoria.

'Yes, quite.'

'You people have no sense of adventure,' grumbled Kimaya. 'I miss Aman. We would have been tucking into burnt garlic-fried rice by now.'

'Is that what they're serving?' asked Aabir, peering out of the window.

'I don't know! I just feel like they're the sort of people who would serve burnt garlic-fried rice. And besides, it sounds delicious.'

Aabir chuckled. 'You're a funny one. Let's go.'

'What!' exclaimed Victoria.

'I resent being accused of being unadventurous. Let's sail in, make a quick demolition of the goods and sail out again. Speed of light.'

Aabir watched Kimaya's face light up with that wide-mouthed grin and decided he'd put the right foot forward.

Victoria drew out a chair and sat down firmly. 'I'm not crashing any godforsaken weddings in this godforsaken country. I'm going to sit here and order myself a martini.'

Aabir was rather taken aback at this outburst; Victoria rarely ever lost her composure in public. 'That's rather mean, Vic.'

'If you call me that again, Aabir, I will *shatter* a glass over your head.'

'Oh, let's go. Let the girl have her martini,' said Kimaya, angrily, pulling Aabir away. 'We have weddings to crash.'

❧

Durgesh sensed crackling tension in the car as he drove the ladies home from Taj Bengal. Or perhaps they'd had one too many glasses of that drink called wine rich people liked. Durgesh himself was the greatest advocate of country liquor. Nothing like a pint of some old-fashioned rural elixir to get one sozzled for the night.

Though Victoria had certainly had more glasses of martini than she cared to count, Kimaya had had nothing to drink. There had been no burnt garlic-fried rice, but a variety of fish and pork that she and Aabir had shamelessly tucked into. An old gentleman had even sidled up to them to strike up a conversation that Aabir had handled fairly well. Kimaya, her heart in her mouth, had replied in monosyllables and Aabir had ragged her later.

'Not so adventurous now, are you?' he'd whispered, as they went back for second helpings of the berry cheesecake parfait.

Before she could answer, a voice had cut in.

'Do I know you from somewhere?'

While Kimaya blanched, Aabir had looked up quizzically. 'Perhaps the pet shop?'

'Pet shop?'

'I own a pet shop on Camac Street. Did you buy a Golden Labrador last month?'

'No, I most certainly didn't. I hate dogs.'

'Then perhaps the parakeet last week?'

'Of course not!'

'White rabbits?'

The gentleman had turned away while Kimaya choked on some parfait.

Aabir winked at her and if she had been any younger, that would have been her undoing. But older and more put-together Kimaya wolfed down dessert, clasped the bride's hands and told her she looked gorgeous, while Aabir solemnly patted the groom on his back and then the two of them had fled as inconspicuously as they could.

'There is *no* pet shop on Camac Street,' hooted Kimaya, after they had put a fair distance between themselves and the poolside wedding.

'He's not likely to check. He hates dogs.'

'You were brilliant!'

'That'll teach you to call me unadventurous!' said Aabir, flicking her cheek.

Kimaya had turned away, her cheeks flushed with the thrill of it all.

'Victoria!' said Aabir, bringing her down to reality. 'We should join her!'

She fought the surge of prejudice that rose within and followed him to the restaurant. They had found Victoria leaning intimately across the table to listen to what a very good-looking young man was saying. When they reached her side, they caught the last strains of French.

'My friends are here,' said Victoria, looking up. Kimaya saw the sparkle in her blue eyes disappear almost immediately.

Victoria introduced them to Raphael, who was here to soak

in the beauty of India. 'So many traditions, so many cultures, so much to learn,' said Raphael, with dramatic gestures.

Aabir and Kimaya had exchanged a glance as they'd drawn up their chairs. Often Victoria and Raphael would break off into rapid French of which Aabir understood little and Kimaya understood none. When Kimaya had started yawning, Raphael had offered to drive Victoria home later that night.

'I don't think that will be necessary,' Aabir had said, firmly.

Raphael had looked offended and Victoria, disconcerted. 'I'm sure he means well,' she had whispered, fervently.

'I'm quite sure *well* is not what's on his mind,' Aabir had whispered back.

And an unwilling Victoria had been escorted to the car. Raphael had not tried to take her number. He had not even accompanied her to the main door.

When the car rolled to a halt at the gates of Kimaya's house, Durgesh leapt out and held the door open for Victoria. Victoria struggled to gather up the pleats of her saree and he held out a hand, offering assistance.

'Why is he offering me his hand?' hissed Victoria. 'Tell him to take it away.'

'Victoria!' cried an outraged Kimaya.

Victoria looked stricken for a moment before her features arranged itself in an icy composure. Kimaya slammed the door shut and stalked inside. Self-control was not a forte, but rage had rendered her speechless.

There was no one to surrender to Pepper's exuberance that night. Tanuja watched in unobtrusive curiosity as bedroom doors slammed shut for the night.

Chapter Twenty-one

Narayan had lost his customary affability. He watched The Holy One stab a podgy finger into the spongy rasgolla, to test its freshness, and muttered darkly.

'So how is your daughter doing, Narayan? Any progress?'

'I don't think so.'

'I see. And how long do you plan to keep her there?'

'Until she has performed her duty.'

'Oh. Mrs Mookerjee is pleased with her work.'

'Good.'

'I don't think she should get too comfortable there.'

'Oh?'

'She may not want to come back.'

'Oh.'

There was a pause, filled by the corpulent sound of the purohit swallowing a rasgolla.

'Geeta heard you telling Mrs Mookerjee that you have found a suitable girl for her son.'

'I may have,' said Purohitmoshai, guardedly.

'And you don't think that that is a breach of our agreement?' snarled Narayan.

'Our agreement was that we share the profits of the jewel if your daughter finds it. We did not agree that I would stop looking for a bride for Aabir Mookerjee.'

'And what happens if Aabir weds one of these suitable girls?'

Purohitmoshai looked surprised. 'Why, then the emerald will be gifted to me, of course.'

Babloo, standing beside his father, flexed his biceps menacingly.

'And you think you can get away with this?' shouted Narayan. Other customers looked up startled. They were not used to a holy man being mistreated by a mere commoner.

'Of course,' replied the purohit, beatifically.

'I will see you in hell,' threatened Narayan, blinded by rage. He did not see Mukul enter the shop and stop short at the commotion.

'What is wrong with you?' asked a gentleman. 'You cannot speak in this manner to a man of God!'

'We are not coming back to this shop,' said a woman, stalking out.

'But Ma,' protested her young son, 'their sweets are better than anyone else's!'

Babloo drew his father inside and Purohitmoshai elephantined out. He was sure the last girl was going to make the cut. The emerald would be his.

❧

The door burst open and Aabir sat up with a yelp.

'Wake *up*, it's an emergency!'

Aabir blinked at a dark shadow framed against his bedroom door and desperately groped for his phone. It glowed—6.15 a.m. He stared wildly at the figure flinging aside curtains to let in the early morning sun. There, outlined against his window, was the passionate person of Rana Raina.

'Gghhh,' said Aabir, eloquently. Much to the chagrin of his mother, he had never been a morning person. He had never suspected Rana Raina of belonging to that inexplicable breed either, but here he was, hollering in his room in the middle of the night. Why had anyone let him in, is what Aabir wanted to know.

'Oh wake *up*, will you? Lump!'

'How...what...why?' spluttered Aabir, his hair standing on end.

Mukul looked timidly into the room. No one had ever dared to wake up Aabirda in such an unseemly fashion.

'Good morning, Mukul,' said Rana Raina, cheerfully. 'I'd like an egg-white omelette. And sausages if you have them. Make them oily. And oh, a slice of brown bread. Skip the butter.'

Mukul looked at Aabir, who still looked like a man whose

heart had leapt out of his mouth and hadn't found its way back in yet.

'Tea. Ginger,' he croaked.

Mukul sidled away and Rana Raina drew up a chair beside the bed. He sat down and propped his legs up on the bed.

'This room hasn't changed a bit,' he said, looking around. 'Can't remember the last time I was here. Your sixteenth birthday I think.'

Aabir sat up in bed and set a pillow against the headboard.

'Are you dying?' he asked, shortly.

Rana Raina looked surprised. 'Who, me? Course not. Far from it. Fit as a fiddle.'

An imperceptible growl escaped Aabir's throat.

'Be nice,' said Rana Raina, lighting a cigarette.

Aabir reached across the bed and snatched away the cigarette. 'No smoking in this room!'

Rana Raina shrugged. 'I'm going to do it. It's happening tonight.'

'Who? What?' Aabir was not quick on the uptake when his brain was still slumbering.

'I'm going to ask her to marry me.'

'Who! What!' Aabir felt his brain waking up. It was protesting.

'I'm going to,' said Rana Raina, lighting another cigarette, 'ask Mia to marry me.'

Aabir made an unintelligible sound and removed the second cigarette from his friend's mouth.

'It feels *right*. It's the only way I'll ever have her.'

Even in his hebetude, new-found respect for Mia Chatterjee dawned on Aabir. That little vixen had had the winning hand all this time. He struggled out of bed and wobbled towards Rana Raina and shook him by the shoulder.

'I know, I know. It's time to celebrate.'

'No! You idiot! This is what she wants! She wants you to marry her and she's been playing mind games all this time!'

'Well, I want her too, so this is good news. What mind games?'

'Making it look like she's interested in me…that Vedic Village non-shenanigan…'

'She won't be interested in you for long,' said Rana Raina, confidently.

'She's *not*. Why aren't you *listening*?'

'I am. Don't yell,' said Rana Raina, crossly. 'I've had a long hard night. Drank way too much.'

'In the middle of the week?'

'There was a party. Anyway. It hit me over the fourteenth peg. I'm going to ask her to marry me. Tonight. I have it all planned out. I even have a ring in mind.'

'What!' shouted Aabir, very awake.

Mukul, bringing in the breakfast tray, looked startled. Aabir reached weakly for his tea. If Azim had forgotten sugar in the ginger tea *yet* again…and of course he had…

'MUKUL!' roared Aabir.

Rana Raina jumped and dropped his toast. 'Why must you *yell*?' he asked, annoyed.

'No. Sugar.' said Aabir, in measured tones.

'I'll tell Azim, Aabirda.'

'Tell him to hang himself!'

'Yes, Aabirda.'

'Not a morning person, are you?' grinned Raina Raina,

who had recovered from Aabir's unexpected bellow.

Aabir, nibbling on a cookie, glared at him.

'Save one for me. I rather like Mrs Fields.'

'All right, Raina. Now listen to me. You're a beastly person and you have more money than you know what to do with, but I can't let you walk into a death-trap like this. You *can't* marry her!'

'Why not?'

'Because!' spluttered Aabir. 'Well, for one thing, I suspect she is of dubious character.'

'I'm of dubious character.'

'She'll stop at nothing to have her way.'

'I'll stop at nothing to have my way.'

'She's always the subject of scandalous rumours.'

'There's only one thing worse than being talked about; not being talked about.'

'Stop misquoting Oscar Wilde to me at this ungodly hour. Is she older than you? Not that it matters...'

Rana Raina broke into a grin. 'Hell, yeah. I like them older these days.'

'Of course you do.'

'I'm going to put it in the dessert.'

'What? Which?'

'The ring. I'm going to put it in the dessert. Hey, you should come!'

'What! Where?'

Rana Raina smacked his thigh. 'It's an idea! Let's all go for dinner. You bring the hot baker and the British bitch. Mia will never suspect a thing. And then when dessert comes to her...*voila!*'

'And where is this shenanigan happening?'

'Cal Club dining room.'

Aabir spluttered. 'Cal Club! Do you want all the fogeys there to have a joint apoplectic fit?'

'I need Sabir's help. I need him to put the ring in.'

'He works in the library, not the kitchen.'

'So? He has bearer friends, doesn't he?'

Aabir shook his head.

'Dinner at eight. Dress well.'

'I'm always dressed well, you prick.'

Rana Raina finished breakfast and leapt to his feet. 'All right, I have a ring to buy and sleep to catch up on.'

'What ring is this?'

'Something I saw her admiring once. A solitaire set in platinum. I might have trouble explaining it to my dad, but we'll see about that later.'

Aabir spluttered.

'That's a lot of newspapers your sister is carrying,' said Rana Raina, looking out of the window.

Aabir lay down and closed his eyes. 'Just leave, Raina. Leave.'

Rana Raina paused at the door. 'I know she's not perfect, Aabir. But you love who you love and sometimes it's not a choice.'

Chapter Twenty-two

It was midnight and there was only one other customer in E&B—a well-dressed gentleman who was buttering his toast with intent.

'It's even cozier here at night,' said Kimaya, sipping a cup of coffee.

Aabir played absently with the sugar pot.

'I can't believe that ass is engaged. It's not going to last a day, mark my words.'

'Don't be mean, Aabir. I think she was genuinely happy, even if she did have to play games. Meenakshi's always been like that with boys. It's who she is. Even in school she had a bevy of boys around her.'

'Of course she's happy. She's snagged one of the richest men in town, not to mention some of his powerful contacts. But Raina's not half as wily as his dad. He's shown absolutely no interest in politics.'

'I like him.'

'I like him too. He's all heart. Idiotic, but has never hurt a fly. Well, he's hurt women, but discounting that you know...' Aabir broke off, confused.

Kimaya laughed. 'I know. I think the entire ring-in-the-pudding was epic. I'm glad you thought of photographing the moment.'

'Everyone was looking,' mumbled Aabir. 'Don't know why I let myself get talked into these things.'

'Because you're a crème brûlée.'

'And here I was labouring under the impression that I am a man.'

Kimaya giggled. 'You're all gooey inside with this crusty exterior.'

'Please stop.'

Kimaya chuckled. 'Fine. But I think over-the-top gestures are sweet. To know that the other person went through all the trouble of planning a rigmarole just for you, is comforting.'

'But you don't always have to be theatrical to be sincere!' exclaimed Aabir.

'No, you don't. But it's the theatrics that you remember. Aman asked me to marry him when we went snorkelling in the Andamans. At least ten of us were on holiday and we'd all taken a glass-bottomed boat to one of the islands. And suddenly, in the middle of that flora and fauna under the water, he whips out a ring and signals to me. I very nearly stopped breathing.'

'That is quite a story,' said Aabir.

Kimaya looked a little sad. 'So much more interesting than him having popped the question over dinner, no?'

Aabir smiled. 'There might be a certain charm to that if the dinner is special.'

He looked at the serious face before him and took Kimaya's hand. 'I know it's too late in the day to be offering condolences, but I *am* sorry for your loss, Little One.'

Kimaya snorted. 'Who you calling Little One? I'm all of twenty-six.'

'When you're past that wretched beast called thirty, everything that once lay behind it, seems infantile.'

'Even...even great romances of the past?' asked Kimaya, hesitantly.

Aabir looked gravely at her. 'Especially the great romances of the past.'

Kimaya sighed and then blushed when she realized her hand were still under his clasp. She disengaged it and held the mug instead, averting her eyes from Aabir's face and taking a deep interest in her coffee. It occurred to her that when a man started to grow on a girl, it became nearly impossible not to notice excruciating details about him. Like the fact that Aabir's hands were large and warm, and it felt rather good to have her own nestled under his. And when he looked solemn, as he did now, the line of his jaw tightened, which made him very much the Byronic hero. Kimaya was almost afraid to meet his eyes, in case she was unable to conceal her sentiments.

'I wish Vic had come with us tonight,' she said, hurriedly. 'She's determined to be unpleasant.'

Aabir sighed. 'She's not unpleasant, you know. I'll take her out to lunch tomorrow.'

It was the entire manner in which he said it, humbly and yet firmly. Kimaya didn't feel slighted in the least.

'Mocambo,' she said. 'She should at least like *that*. Perhaps a ham steak to lift her mood?'

Aabir looked at her appreciatively. Few things were more

attractive than a woman who was large-hearted enough to allow a man to buy a former paramour a ham steak. Or perhaps it didn't disturb her in the least. Aabir frowned. What if he had misjudged the look in her eye for a passion that was nothing more than the ardour of friendship? The thought made his heart sink. What was it that that Pragya woman had asked him near the pumpkin patch? Had he been soul-crushingly in love with someone? He'd thought of Victoria of course. But now, here he was, his soul asphyxiating him again in a way he hadn't thought was possible.

Aabir reached for Kimaya's hand, and when her fingers trembled a little before steadying themselves, he was assured that his grand gesture would not be in vain.

⤷∽◦

There comes a moment in the lives of all men when they feel that they need to buckle down to the task at hand because the universe has contrived to present a fair spectacle of 'signs' that they can no longer ignore. Aabir Mookerjee felt quite certain that his time for buckling down had arrived, and to put off this act of gallantry that women all over the world swooned for—Disney movies had minted a fortune over this phenomenon—would be cowardice. And Aabir Mookerjee, though lacking the blatant machismo of some of his peers, was no coward. Still, it is not dastardly to lose sleep on the eve of a grand event, especially when one is going to put oneself at the risk of being crushed like a bold but unfortunate mosquito. It has been observed that women set great store by the exquisiteness of the moment and, without a moment's consideration for the man who has spent hours (or weeks if he is the brooding sort) of indigestion over this, will quell a man's dreams if the precise sublimity of the moment has fallen short of her expectations.

In his tense restlessness, Aabir Mookerjee reached for the only substance that would calm his harrowed nerves—his stock of emergency dark chocolate, concealed from his sister's gluttony. Aabir and his sister were both shameless connoisseurs of chocolate and did not hesitate to pinch from the other's stock. Throughout their childhood they had made a game of trying to ferret out each other's hidden candy and, while Aatreyee was more careless with her carefully selected chocolates, Aabir guarded his with all the jealous fierceness of a Rottweiler protecting his bone.

Aabir paced the terrace as he unwrapped his chocolate.

'Oh, stop fretting. It's going to be all right.'

Aabir squinted at the coconut tree. Thakuma yawned.

'Watching you pace about like that is making me dizzy.'

'Oh, right. You live on a tree and the sight of a man walking on solid ground makes you dizzy.'

Thakuma chuckled. 'A man who can retain his sense of humour under pressure has nothing to worry about.'

'I don't think a sense of humour is going to ensure success in this case, Thakuma.'

'You'd be surprised,' said Thakuma, sardonically. 'More women have succumbed to some well-phrased banter than they have to sentimental slush.'

'And were you one of them?' grinned Aabir. He remembered his grandfather had had the uncanny ability to defuse a tense situation with some timely wit.

'Let's just say that the clandestine journey from Chittagong to Calcutta would have been a lot more nerve-wracking had it not been for your grandfather's ceaseless puns.'

Aabir took a thoughtful bite of chocolate.

'You've chosen well. She's a dependable sort, that girl. Which is more than I can say about your last dalliance.'

'Victoria? Don't be hard on her, Thakuma. When I knew her, she was dazzling. I was the luckiest man on campus.'

'Dazzling does not a good wife make.'

'No, but…you love who you love and sometimes it's not a choice.' Aabir was surprised to find himself quoting Rana Raina.

'Oh, I see some of that Raina boy's philosophies have rubbed off.'

'Do you know he's gone and got himself engaged to a woman he barely knows?'

'That boy has a reckless zest for life that is both admirable and absurd.'

'I'm not going to ask Kimaya to marry me just yet, though.'

Thakuma let out a bark of laughter. 'Of course not! I'm not a fool like your feather-brained mother…'

'Er…'

'…to believe that leaping into some wretched marriage is going to be the key to everyone's happiness.'

Aabir chortled. His imperious grandmother—for all her old-school principles—could be surprisingly avant garde.

'You court that girl like she deserves to be courted, Aabir. And she'll shake some of that stuffiness out of you.'

'Hey!'

'Don't *hey* your grandmother. It'll do you good to kick up your heels sometimes.'

Aabir thought of the wedding he had crashed, and smiled.

'I like this one. And besides, anyone who can bake a solid chocolate cake can be depended upon to make a trusty companion.'

Aabir was not sure that the logic was flawless, but it was a theory he wanted to believe in.

'I hope you're right, Thakuma,' he murmured.

'I'm always right,' said Thakuma, fading into the night. 'Always. Right.'

Chapter Twenty-three

Victoria Young felt Aabir's gaze on her as she skimmed the menu in Mocambo. She knew that neither her French braid nor her white dress would go unheeded by him. And indeed it had not. Aabir had always been fond of the French braid as it afforded a clear view of Victoria's elegant neck. Neither had he forgotten the white dress she had on now, which he noticed hung a little loose on her than when she had first worn it to a brunch hosted by one of her cousins. He hadn't realized then that while he had been mesmerized by the simple sophistication of his girlfriend, her father had been regarding, with horror, brown skin resting against classic white.

'We'll start with the devilled crabs and then you can go on to the fish a la diana.'

'I'm not hungry.'

'You will be when the food arrives looking delicious,' said Aabir, cheerfully.

Victoria shrugged.

'I wish you'd been there at dinner last night. No end to the amusement. Rings in the pudding and all that. Do you remember Rana Raina from the time he visited me in England?'

'Vaguely.'

'He went and proposed to this girl—an acquaintance of Kimaya's from school actually—in the club dining room and all the waiters gathered about to watch when the dessert was served. So of course all the members had to peer around to see what the fuss was for. It was quite embarrassing.'

'I see.'

Aabir sighed. 'You seem out of sorts, Victoria.'

'It's the weather.'

The weather was not blameless, thought Victoria. It could bring anyone down, even someone who hadn't been forced to realize that she could no longer bring a former lover to his knees with simply a glance. When she caught his gaze over the low-hanging lantern, she was taken aback by how little he had changed. Not that he was rake thin anymore, but his hair was parted in the same manner, his nose still quivered in annoyance when the man at the next table bellowed into his phone and he still used the pale blue handkerchief with the single A on it, monogrammed in white. In a world where friends dropped you like hot cakes, lovers pledged eternal fidelity before disappearing and mothers abandoned their children with less than competent fathers, the enduring habits of Aabir Mookerjee provided solace. And yet, when she looked up, she found him frowning at something over her shoulder. Her Abe would have been studying the arch of her head and would have smiled when she looked up. Her Abe would not have forgotten that she hated facing a wall when she was seated at a restaurant. Her Abe would not have crashed a wedding dinner with another woman.

A sinking heart informed Victoria that the Aabir

Mookerjee who sat before her now, trying to make her comfortable and draw her out of her thoughts, was no longer her Abe, and that she had lost him, perhaps irretrievably, when she had been unable to defend him against the odds—the way she should have, the way he would have, had the tables been turned.

'It's more than just the weather, isn't it?'

The men she met these days lacked the keen emotional intelligence that Aabir had come so well equipped with. He had always picked up on her subtle signs, whether she talked too fast or too little, too loudly or too soft. He had known when to prod her for an answer and when to let her stew. He had even let a white lie or two pass, but sometimes he had called her out.

She looked him in the eye. His apparent concern melted some of her petulance. 'I've lost you, haven't I?'

If he was taken aback by her bluntness, he didn't let it show. 'I thought we'd lost each other a couple of years ago.'

'Perhaps not as irrevocably then as we have now.'

'I think I realized the inevitability of the rift before you did, Victoria.'

She wanted to weep at the kindness in his voice, the gentility of his manner. If only her father could have had the foresight to have seen that nobility was so much more than a seat in the House of Lords. If only she had had the strength to not be petrified at the threat of losing all she had been used to. She turned her head and saw the guard mopping his brow in the blazing sun, a semi-clad woman setting a bawling baby down on the broken pavement across the road and she was glad that she would soon be on a flight back to an environment that did not continually assault her senses.

'I think I'll order the fish a la diana,' she told Aabir.

'Excellent choice,' he grinned. He had chosen not to probe the topic.

'I'm afraid I've behaved rather badly with Kimaya.'

'And what are you going to do about it?'

'Apologize profusely?'

'Right.'

'Do you have something in mind?'

Aabir hesitated. 'No...not particularly.'

Victoria looked at him. 'I know you like her, Abe.'

'And just how do you know that? I didn't realize myself until last night, and even then I needed my grandmother to make some incisive points.'

'When a woman has been intimate with a man, she recognizes his surreptitious glance and a particular tilt of his head, even when it's not directed at her. This is why men should think twice before having an affair.'

Aabir laughed. 'I think your historical romance is going to do just fine.'

'Thank you. I hope so. Now tell me what it is you want me to do.'

'Have you seen *Alice in Wonderland*?'

'Tim Burton?'

'Walt Disney.'

'A long time ago.'

Aabir leaned in. 'There's a scene...'

And Victoria heard him out, in part delight and part envy. And in the end she sighed. If only...

Nobody, in this world or the next, enjoyed being proven right as gleefully as Thakuma did. In the days of flesh and blood, she had had a way of cocking her eyebrows at her husband in a manner that screamed *I told you so* more maddeningly than words. And had her husband shared her leafy abode, she would have cocked her eyebrows again for Geeta had not been snooping around the house lately. In fact, as far as Thakuma could see—and Thakuma could see everything—she had been working very meticulously indeed. She followed Azim around like a dog, even when he was trying to read the newspapers in the evening, and he had looked up and glared at the coconut tree in exasperation.

Eighteen is an age full of conundrums. By the law one is an adult, and yet it is difficult to behave sensibly all the time. If one attempts to be wiser than one is, one is put in one's place, but if one gives in to any sort of petulance, one is reproached for being childish. Eighteen-year-old Geeta was not enjoying the contradictions of her age. She had been rebuked by her father for being lazy, even though she had tried to explain that it was no easy task, and besides, she had a lot of work and little time to explore the house.

'Stop being a child, Geeta. We all have work. Don't forget what you have been sent there to do.'

'Are you sure you didn't misunderstand the police, Baba? I can't imagine anyone in that house stealing, you know. Everyone is so honest, I feel ashamed. And why can't the police just come themselves?'

'Stop asking questions about things that are none of your business, you stupid girl, and do as you're told,' Babloo had said, flicking her ear.

That same afternoon Geeta watched Azim store away a small amount of left-over rice into the fridge, after Mrs Mookerjee and Aatreyee had finished dinner, and serve Mukul, Geeta and himself the thicker, cheaper variety of rice. Azim was clearly the sole proprietor of the kitchen. Mrs Mookerjee had not thought it necessary to continue Thakuma's iron regime and let the servants have the run of the place. As long as the job was getting done, Mrs Mookerjee did not concern herself with the daily humdrum of housekeeping. It had not stopped to amaze Geeta that the man never pilfered from the larder. Not once had she seen him sneak out even an almond for himself, and here she was trying to rob the family of something precious.

When everyone had crawled into their respective beds for the customary post-lunch shut-eye, Geeta lay on her mattress and stared up at the wood-panelled ceiling of her room. Slowly, she began to put two and two together. Her brother had been angry when he had heard that Purohitmoshai had been looking for brides for Aabir and she knew that Boudi had offered him an expensive gift. Mukul had told her that she had seen her father arguing with the purohit the next day and now her father wanted her to hurry up and find the ring. Geeta sat up in bed, her heart racing. It was all a nasty plot, she realized. Her father must want the ring that had been promised to Purohitmoshai and they were fighting about it. Geeta got up and started pacing the room. What was she to do? Could she tell Aabirda? What if he took her to the police? What if he took her father to the police? Perhaps she could plead with her father to see sense; she knew he was not a bad man.

Geeta sat down again. She wished she had never stolen anything in her life. She wished she had not stolen that doll from her friend in school when she was six. And fifty rupees from her father when she was eleven. And fish fry from the vendor at the Durga Puja pandal when she was sixteen. She had even stolen jackfruit from the Mookerjees not so long ago! Geeta wished she had been like Azim; no one would even dream of asking Azim to steal something, not even his own father. Suddenly, Geeta remembered all the things she had hidden under her mattress and fell to her knees with a cry. She rummaged out the gold paperclips, the pretty envelope that she had found in the large room with so many bookshelves, the butterfly-shaped safety pin that Boudi sometimes used to pin up her saree. God was punishing her for being a deceitful little sneak. And Azim...Azim would be so ashamed of her. How would she ever face him again? He would be repulsed by her duplicity, and of course she would be sent away and no decent family would ever hire her again.

Geeta turned to her side and sobbed into her pillow. Thakuma nodded in approval; a little repentance never did anyone any harm. Any moment now these fools would all out-do each other and their little game would explode around them. Thakuma even let out an un-ladylike snigger. Being dead was so much more fun than being alive.

Chapter Twenty-four

In the first throes of love, when nothing has been admitted or confirmed and everything is non-committal, one undergoes periods of misgiving or certainty, ecstasy or misery, and sometimes, very inconveniently, all sorts of heightened emotion together. Kimaya found herself in exactly such a tiresome spot. That morning Mia Chatterjee had sailed in to place an order for fifty bacon scones and another seventy chocolate tortes that made Kimaya have second thoughts about having written her off as an insufferable cat in school. At least until Mia had looked up and leaned over conspiratorially and said, 'So, are you instrumental in bringing the old lovers together?'

'What are you talking about?' said Kimaya, startled.

'You know…that beautiful white girl I saw Aabir kissing in Flurys.'

Kimaya had frozen. 'You *saw*…'

'Oh, everyone saw. They were standing right there in the middle of Flurys. Of course, all the men must have been jealous. I'm glad my Rana prefers flamboyance to boring simplicity.'

'I wasn't aware that Rana Raina had any strict preferences,'

Kimaya said, unable to swallow her anger, and Mia Chatterjee had walked out in a bit of a huff.

But Kimaya spent the next couple of hours letting her imagination and appetite run wild. With every gingerbread man that she ate, she imagined Aabir creeping just a little closer to his golden-haired princess until there was no bridling their passion, not even the presence of the other patrons of Flurys. Just when a gingerbread leg tasted particularly good and she convinced herself that Aabir Mookerjee was not the kind to deceive a woman, the image of Victoria pressed up against the make-believe three-tiered cake in the centre of Flurys led to the demolishment of two hapless gingerbread heads. When Victoria walked into the house, she found Kimaya looking dejectedly at a piece of round white chocolate, the only evidence that gingerbread men with white buttons had once lain on the porcelain plate.

'I never eat gingerbread men,' said Kimaya. 'It feels so cruel.'

Victoria was amused. 'And yet you eat fish and goats and pigs and…'

'Oh, put a lid on it, will you?' snapped Kimaya, flouncing out of the room.

But Kimaya Kapoor was not a woman to let her passions get the better of her for long, so when Victoria pleaded with her to wrap up early because it was her last night in town, she agreed, albeit reluctantly. They had just decided on an early dinner at the Oberoi Grand, when the odd-job boy came tearing up the stairs to report that an old lady in South End Park had ordered for ten pots of crème brûlée and had asked if the young lady would deliver it herself that evening;

she had heard so much about her.

'Absurd!' exclaimed Kimaya. 'She can't possibly expect ten pots of crème brûlée this evening when she ordered it just now.'

'Old women can be irrational,' murmured Victoria.

The odd-job boy mumbled something about how the order had been placed two days ago and he had clean forgotten about it. Kimaya leapt up in agitation.

'What do we do now? Do we even have ten pots of crème brûlée?'

The odd-job boy confirmed that they did.

'You might as well go, you know. She probably just wants to see who's running this absurd confectionery. You'll charm her, don't worry. Just wear something nice.'

'Oh please. She's a batty old woman,' said Kimaya, dismissively.

'And she lived in an era where outward appearance was much more important than it is now.'

Kimaya chewed her lip. 'I guess I could wear the shirt you brought me.'

'Instead, why don't you wear that blue and white dress I brought you?'

'Oh no! I was saving that for something much more eventful than playing delivery girl.'

'You won't have to change for dinner, then, and my leaving is such an event!'

Kimaya chuckled. 'No really, I...'

'And I do want to see you in that dress. I debated over it a long time.'

'Oh, all right, all right.'

'Alice,' murmured Victoria, giving the odd-job boy the

thumbs up behind Kimaya's back. He grinned back at her cheekily.

'What are you grinning at?' said Kimaya, sternly. 'Mess up any more orders like this and I'll slash your wages.'

The odd-job boy looked penitent, but Kimaya did not feel charitable towards him. She felt even less charitable when she went around in circles looking for 334 South End Park, and when she found it after an hour—Durgesh seemed particularly slow that evening—an empty plot of land between 333 and 335. She stared at it stupefied and rang the odd-job boy in a fluster. He said the incensed old lady had cancelled the order because it hadn't been delivered on time and seemed surprised that Kimaya was standing before 334 South End Park when he had clearly stated 334 Jodhpur Park.

Kimaya hung up in a fine temper. Idiotic boy! Mrs Mookerjee had been right to fire the imbecile. How dare Aabir foist this fool on her! How exasperating of Victoria to insist she wear this dress. Kimaya decided she'd had enough of everyone. She would call the old lady and apologize tomorrow, but today she was going to cancel all plans and watch a movie in bed. *Notting Hill* always cheered her up. No, no romances. Maybe just some episodes of *Friends* instead.

The traffic she incurred on her way back home did nothing to improve Kimaya's mood and she was about to stalk up to her apartment when she noticed the lights on in the ground floor. She even heard singing! The odd-job boy was having a little party, was he? She'd give him something to sing about. She flung open the door.

'What...' she began, angrily and then stopped short.

It seemed one of her waiters, still dressed as a Mad Hatter, had company. 'A very merry unbirthday to me...' she was singing.

Victoria!

'To who?'

Aabir Mookerjee!

'To me!'

'Oh you!'

'A very merry unbirthday to you!'

'Who, me?'

'Yes, you!'

'Oh, me!'

Kimaya stared at Victoria's red coat and bow tie in amazement. The Mad Hatter and the March Hare? What were those two up to?

'Let's all congratulate us with another cup of tea. A very merry unbirthday to u-u-uss!' they warbled.

Kimaya looked down at her blue-and-white summer dress and realization struck her. She tip-toed across the room and sat down at the head of the long table that had been created by shifting everything around.

'Now, it's very very rude to sit down without being invited,' said Aabir, fixing her with a glare.

'I'm very sorry, but I did enjoy your singing,' said Kimaya, who knew the script perfectly.

'You enjoyed *our* singing?' asked Victoria, the March Hare, surprised.

'Oh what a delightful child! You must have a cup of tea.'

'Ah, yes, indeed. You must have a cup of tea!' the March Hare agreed fervently, pouring some tea into a little pink porcelain cup.

'That would be very nice. I'm sorry if I interrupted your birthday party,' said Kimaya, very Alice-like.

'Birthday?' cackled the March Hare. 'My dear child, this is not a birthday party!'

'Of course not! This is an unbirthday party,' chortled the Mad Hatter.

'Unbirthday? I'm sorry but I don't quite understand...'

'Good God, the girl doesn't know what an unbirthday is! I'm not sure I can stand around to witness her ignorance!' exclaimed the March Hare, picking up a strawberry muffin and sweeping into the kitchen.

'What was that?' said Kimaya, surprised. 'That's not part of the script.'

'An unbirthday is when there isn't a birthday to celebrate,' said Aabir, taking off his top hat.

'Yes, yes. Every day is an unbirthday, but...'

'And sometimes it's grand-gesture day.'

'Huh?'

'When you make a grand gesture to show that you care,' said Aabir, leaning against the table.

Kimaya went very white.

'W...what do you mean?'

'You're like red velvet cheesecake, Kimaya Kapoor. You surprise me all the time. So here's my grand gesture.'

'You're as mad as a Hatter!'

'I suspect that has something to do with you.'

Kimaya wanted the butterflies in her stomach to just settle down for a moment so this could all sink in.

'Without further ado, madamoiselle, you might as well put me out of my misery and let me know whether or not you will agree to be my exclusive red velvet cheesecake.'

Kimaya began to laugh. 'You're terrible at this, aren't you?'

Aabir flushed and removed his green coat. 'I am. I'm sorry. I don't know what I was thinking. I fear I've made a frightful ass of myself and...'

He couldn't complete his sentence because Kimaya flung herself on him. His last coherent thought, before her lips descended on his, was that she smelt of strawberries and cinnamon.

Chapter Twenty-five

While humming along with Eine Kleine Nachtmusik, Aabir Mookerjee stopped to sniff the air around him. He followed the smell to his wrists and realized with alarm that he smelt of The Mad Hatter bakery and hastily reached for his Burberry pour homme. Brushing his hair, he surveyed the set of clothes that he had had Mukul lay out for him. He held up the white shirt with the baby blue-dress stripes and decided that this was just the occasion to wear it. He had bought it with the intention of wearing it to Victoria's twenty-seventh birthday party, but it was an event that he had never attended and thus the shirt had never been worn.

'Special occasion, isn't it, Churchill?' said Aabir, fondly, and the dog immediately rolled over in drooling assent. It was not often that his master entertained ladies at home and two together was unprecedented. Churchill thumped his tail in delight at this sudden development.

The previous night, after Aabir had discarded his borrowed Mad Hatter costume, he and Kimaya had spent hours curled up in each other's arms on the window seat that overlooked the hustle and bustle of Calcutta, talking of everything and talking of nothing. Aabir couldn't remember the last time he had been quite so happy. Not that he had been unhappy of course, but the inexplicable comfort of being in the company of a person who simply *understood*, was a rarity he had forgotten. It was the kind of contentment he had taken for granted once and had been painfully forced to realize that 'tis a treasure not easily replicable. Near about midnight they had awoken Victoria and had set out in Aabir's car to take her around the city where, in the cool night air and absence of noise and chaos, Victoria began to appreciate, for the first time, the quaint beauty of Calcutta. In a moment of exuberance, she had asked to meet Aabir's family before she left for London the next day and Aabir had insisted that they both land up for lunch, since few things gave his mother as much joy as entertaining house guests who she could plague with tales of her good-for-nothing children.

There was a discreet knock on Aabir's bedroom door. That would be Mukul, sent up to tell him that breakfast was served. *Every morning*. Aabir decided to overlook his mother's regular interruption of his morning toilette; it was a glorious day and the sky was just the right kind of cerulean, definitely not the kind of cerulean conducive to irritability.

'I'll be down in ten minutes,' he told a grinning Mukul, upon opening the door.

'Azim wants to know what your friends would like for lunch today.'

'Oh right. We'll have an early lunch. One of them has a flight to board. She'll have a very bland baked fish and tell him to go easy on the garlic. She dislikes garlic.'

Mukul nodded.

'And the rest of us can have some dal, *aloo bhaja*—make sure they're fine and crispy—and that *kosha mangsho* that he makes.'

Mukul's eyes lit up. It was going to be a good day.

'And Mukul. Tell him that today he must be on top of his game. It is very important, do you understand?'

Mukul grinned widely. He understood perfectly. Aabir shuddered, as he often did, at the range of yellow teeth and shut the door. Perhaps he should send Mukul to a dentist.

Humming softly, he debated whether to be risqué and wear the scarlet pocket square with his teal-blue waistcoat. It might be just the sort of thing that Kimaya would like. She'd probably turn up in a comic little thing herself. Aabir grinned. She stood out, that girl. Perhaps not in the understated elegance that Aabir thought he appreciated in women, but in a cheerful, hearty way. But of course, when one is beautiful and smelt of strawberries and cinnamon, anything one deigned to wear was fashionable. Aabir whistled a tune he hadn't in years and then stopped to survey his merry face in the mirror. By God, it was true! Love had its way of creeping into one's skin and making it glow like a ruddy lamp.

'I feel quite handsome, Churchill, if I may say so myself.'

Churchill barked in acquiescence.

Unfortunately, not all the inhabitants of Mookerjee House were quite as cheery as Aabir that morning. Geeta proceeded to go about her morning chore rather listlessly and if Mrs Mookerjee chose to ignore a lack of efficiency, it was because she was much too excited at her son having invited two females for lunch. By Mrs Mookerjee's calculations, that doubled the chances of a wedding and she rang the purohit, giddy with joy. Needless to say, Purohitmoshai was less than happy that his own candidate had been elbowed out of the competition without so much as a malpua and had wrangled an invitation for himself so he could disparage these lady friends.

When he rolled in corpulently, he heard voices raised in merriment from the garden. With pursed lips he followed the sounds of mirth and paused to watch furtively when he spotted Aabir pouring wine for his guests on the porch that led into the living room.

'May I help you?'

The low, curt voice made Purohitmoshai jump.

'Oh, good morning, good morning. How are you, my dear? I was just going in for lunch. So kind of your mother to always call me when you have guests.'

'Is that so?' replied Aatreyee, her lips set in a thin line.

Purohitmoshai shuffled his feet; this strange young woman always made him uncomfortable. What was *wrong* with these Mookerjees!

'I was looking for your mother,' he said, unable to wipe the beatific smile off his face.

Aatreyee pointed to the porch, where Mrs Mookerjee had emerged with a tray of what was most likely some delicious appetisers.

'Of course, of course. There she is. I'll go meet her, shall I?' Nervous laughter at an icily raised eyebrow. 'I'll see you for lunch, then?'

Cold silence. Purohitmoshai coughed and elephantined his way up the cobbled pathway, fighting the urge to look back to meet the frosty eyes following him.

Not that the eyes that met his were particularly welcoming.

Aabir, in fact, looked distinctly displeased at the sight of his least favourite guest infiltrating his afternoon.

'Why is that man *always* here, Ma?' he growled in a low voice.

Mrs Mookerjee looked up. 'Oh don't be mean, Aabir. He's seen you grow up. You're always rude to him.'

Aabir grunted, loath to be thrown off his high spirits by this unwelcome intrusion. 'Purohitmoshai, Kimaya Kapoor and Victoria Young. Girls, our family priest of sorts.'

'Hello, hello. Very nice to meet you both. I have seen Aabir since he was *so* small. He was as he is now, very serious and always reading. Never went out to play or anything.'

Kimaya laughed. 'I can believe that,' she said, in stilted Bengali. Purohitmoshai frowned at her as he reached out for a cube of *kabiraji*. He studied the way Aabir's eyes rested on her even while he replied to Victoria, and his frown deepened.

'A Punjabi girl, Debjani?' he hissed, following her inside the house. 'Is this what we've come to?'

'She's so pretty but!' exclaimed Mrs Mookerjee, taken aback at the thought that the cheerful Kimaya might be considered unsuitable.

'*Punjabi*! Do you think she will be able to uphold your traditions? Do you think she won't try to cause a rift between you and your son? Do you think...' Purohitmoshai leaned menacingly over the alarmed Mrs Mookerjee, 'that she will be able to make you posto-bora every Saturday?'

Mrs Mookerjee gasped. 'I...I wasn't thinking!'

Purohitmoshai stepped back, disgust writ over his podgy face. 'And you were passing over the Bengali gem I had in mind for our Aabir? Tell me, Debjani, do you even love your son as you claim to? What kind of mother would let such a horrific mistake pass?'

'Oh no, Purohitmoshai, please don't say these things. It never occurred to me...' began Mrs Mookerjee, tears welling up in her eyes. But Purohitmoshai had spun around and was making his grand exit. Raised voices made him pause. In a moment Mukul appeared at the head of the stairs, dragging along a reluctant Geeta.

'Caught her red-handed,' he panted at Mrs Mookerjee, who was hurriedly drying her eyes.

'At what?' asked Mrs Mookerjee.

Purohitmoshai stared.

'Snooping in your room and she put *this* in her pocket!' Mukul held out a silver ring encrusted with green stones.

Mrs Mookerjee fingered the ring and glared at Geeta, 'Thief!' she exclaimed.

Purohitmoshai decided it was time to continue his grand exit.

'It's him!' shrieked Geeta. 'He's been trying to steal your ring!'

Mrs Mookerjee spluttered. Mukul choked.

'How dare you?' shouted Purohitmoshai. 'How dare you accuse me of such things you...you *servant*!'

Aabir strode out of the living room. 'Why are people always *yelling* in this house? Can we attempt to be civilized in front of strangers?'

'He wants the ring,' repeated Geeta, stubbornly, trying to wriggle free from Mukul's vice-like grip on her arm.

'What is she babbling about?' asked Aabir. 'Who wants what ring?'

'Purohitmoshai wants a ring,' explained Mrs Mookerjee.
'Which ring?'

'No ring!' hooted Purohitmoshai.

'A green ring!' cried Geeta. 'He told my father that if I found the old green ring, they could both sell it!'

'Nonsense!' roared Purohitmoshai. 'I'll beat you senseless… I'll…'

'Is she talking about the Hardinge emerald?' asked Aabir of his mother.

Mrs Mookerjee looked bewildered. 'I don't know…but this is just an imitation jewel your sister left lying around in my room,' she held out the silver ring to Aabir who didn't seem inclined to take it.

'I'm talking about the ring that Boudi promised Purohitmoshai if he found Aabirda a suitable wife,' wept Geeta. 'I'm not lying.'

'Ma!' hooted Aabir.

'Rubbish! I haven't promised anyone that emerald!' exclaimed Mrs Mookerjee.

Purohitmoshai's contrived outrage was wiped off his face. 'Eh,' he gasped, 'you promised me the emerald after I had found Aabir a bride.'

'What are you talking about?' snapped Mrs Mookerjee, reaching the end of her tether. 'I promised you the grandfather clock!'

A stunned silence descended on the merry gathering. Thakuma, looking down at the proceedings with glee, was no longer gleeful. That grandfather clock had been sent to her by her eldest brother as a peace offering, five years after she had eloped with Rathindra Mookerjee. And here was her daughter-in-law giving it away to this unspeakably crooked man. She was doing this to get back at her mother-in-law of course. Ungrateful wretch. If Thakuma hadn't been around, God knows what kind of heathens she would have brought up with her irresponsible husband. Thakuma felt fresh rage at her son for having brought home someone as utterly unpleasant as Debjani Mookerjee, née Dasgupta.

'What?' spluttered the purohit.

'Why would you assume I was going to give you a family heirloom?' shouted Mrs Mookerjee. 'You mad man! That old woman was right about you all this time!'

Thakuma didn't know whether to gloat over this late victory or take umbrage to being referred to as 'that old woman'.

'Purohitmoshai,' said Aabir, sternly.

The fat purohit began to back away.

'Where do you think you're going?' asked Aabir, dangerously.

The purohit broke into a fast waddle once more.

'Churchill!' roared Aabir. Churchill, napping in a patch of sunlight in the study, sat up, startled. It wasn't often that his master raised his voice, let alone roar.

'Churchill!'

Churchill was up in a trice and bounding down the stairs.

'Treat!' said Aabir, pointing at the purohit's fast retreating figure.

Churchill knew what that meant! He flew over the centre table—'The rose bowl!' shrieked Mrs Mookerjee—and was almost at Purohitmoshai's ankled. Kimaya and Victoria looked up startled as Aabir's family priest shot into the front porch, crashing into the trolley of kabiraji and lemonade on the way.

'Oh dear, be careful!' cried Victoria, springing to her feet.

Aabir appeared at the door. 'Treat!' he called, angrily.

'What's happening?' asked Kimaya, craning her neck to see Dog and Priest hotfooting it down the garden.

'We're about to find out,' said Aabir, grimly, stalking after them.

The occupants of Mookerjee House were beginning to spill out. Bahadur and the gardener crept around the corner. Geeta was running after Aabir, this time pulling Mukul along with her. And Azim stood on an upturned flower pot in the kitchen garden to have a better view of the hullaballoo. Purohitmoshai had locked himself up in the shed. Churchill was going quite mad, flinging himself against the unyielding door. He cocked his head to listen for a moment before resuming the flinging.

'Down,' said Aabir, arriving at the shed.

Churchill sat down reluctantly, but kept up a low growl.

'Come out, Purohitmoshai. It's no good.'

There was no reply but plenty of scuffling. Aabir turned the handle and was surprised that the door opened. When he spotted the breathless purohit on the floor of the shed, he was even more surprised.

'Puppies!' squealed Victoria and Kimaya in unison.

'Puppies!' spluttered Aabir.

'Puppies!' gurgled Mrs Mookerjee.

Seven puppies gambolled over Purohitmoshai's large person.

'Why is everyone here?' said a cross voice from the corner.

Aabir turned to find his sister squatting on the floor with Lady Mountbatten, both looking more vexed than they usually did. He smacked his forehead. 'It all makes sense! The newspapers and the cushions and the milk!' He looked hurt. 'I can't believe you didn't let me in on this.'

'I will not have more dogs!' shrieked Mrs Mookerjee. 'This is too much!'

'Ole, let me have them,' crooned Kimaya sinking to her knees.

Churchill, sniffing around the purohit, attempted to take a puppy in his mouth and Lady Mountbatten leapt forward snarling. Churchill hurriedly backed away.

All the help began crowding into the shed and the puppies were delighted at all the new human smells. They began to crawl off Purohitmoshai and cavort around the others.

'Where did they come from?' asked Aabir, picking up a puppy and tickling its ear. Churchill whined.

'Rescued them. The mother was run over by a reckless car. Usual story.'

'Their mother is dead, Ma,' said Aabir to his mother. 'They're orphans. How can you be so cruel?'

'This is all your fault!' shouted Mrs Mookerjee. 'If you would just agree to get yourself a wife, none of this would have happened.' She swung around and pushed herself through the congregation of guests, servants and puppies, and marched out of the door.

Aabir looked at Kimaya, mortified. He noticed the corner of her lip trembling and the laughter in her eyes, and held up his hand.

'Don't say it,' he warned. 'Don't you dare say it!'

⌣

Purohitmoshai was not turned away from the lunch table, but for the first time in his life he was not tempted by the tender mutton pieces cooked in velvety-thick gravy. Like a pure-blood Bengali, Aabir agreed with Maslow that a good meal was to be given more importance than law and order, and had summoned for lunch before summoning the police. Geeta was too ashamed to meet Azim, so she had escaped to the terrace to sob into the pots of dahlia that lined the wall.

'Oh, dry up. Nothing's going to happen. My grandson isn't going to fire another servant.'

Geeta leapt up with a cry and looked around. 233

'Here, on the coconut tree, you stupid girl.'

Geeta froze. The rumours were true then! The old woman was indeed residing on the coconut tree! Trembling, Geeta backed up against the wall. Thakuma watched her impatiently.

'What do you think I'm going to do to you?' she said, rolling her eyes.

'I don't know,' whimpered Geeta, terrified.

'Don't be silly. Now listen to me. I'm going to give you a recipe for posto-bora that no one else knows. Make a batch of it and take it to the lunch table.'

Geeta nodded mutely.

'Come closer, you stupid girl!'

In spite of Thakuma's defamation, Geeta was not a stupid girl. While Azim hovered around the guests in the dining room, she whipped up a storm of posto-bora at the speed of light. The secret ingredient had delighted her. Mukul watched, puzzled.

'You were asked to do this?' he repeated every six minutes.

Ignoring him, Geeta carried a platter of poppy-seed kabas out to the dining room. It seemed everyone, except the purohit, had recovered from the morning's unpleasantness.

'Why you were hiding puppies in the shed, I'll never understand,' Mrs Mookerjee was telling her daughter.

'Oh please, Ma,' said Aabir, rising to his sister's defence. 'Like you would have allowed seven mongrel puppies to run around the house.'

'Don't accuse me of discriminating against dogs.'

'You don't. You don't like any of them. But you have to love ours,' said Aabir, tossing Churchill a bone. Mountbatten, surprisingly, had placed her chin on Kimaya's lap. 'Including the two new additions.'

'I liked the white little thing with the brown ears. Dibs on that one,' said Kimaya.

Mrs Mookerjee shuddered. 'Love is carrying it too far. I'm glad we know enough people to take them off our hands.' She turned towards Victoria. 'I hope you like the fish, dear.'

'Yes, very much, thank you,' smiled Victoria. She and Aatreyee had been conversing in an undertone on the other side of the table, much to the concealed bewilderment of Aabir and his mother.

'And I hope you have had an eventful visit to India.'

'Very,' laughed Victoria, catching Aabir's eye. 'I've invited Aatreyee to visit me in London. I think she'll love it.'

'Shall,' agreed Aatreyee.

Before her family had had time to react to this, Geeta

had entered, bearing a platter.

'What's this?' said Mrs Mookerjee.

Azim stared at Geeta, his eyebrows furrowed.

'Some posto-bora,' said Geeta, setting it down in the middle of the table.

Aabir pursed his lips.

'Won't you try one, Aabirda?' asked Geeta.

Azim looked at her in outrage.

'Well, all right,' said Aabir, who didn't want to seem uncharitable. When he bit into the first one, his face lit up. 'Thakuma!' he shouted. 'Thakuma's back!'

'Don't be silly, Aabir,' said Mrs Mookerjee, casting a nervous glance at her puzzled guests.

'Taste it!' exclaimed Aabir, shoving the tray towards his sister.

235

Aatreyee obliged. 'Thakuma,' she confirmed.

'Geeta, who made these?' demanded Aabir.

Geeta looked at Azim's furious face and smiled. 'He did, of course.'

'Azim!' said Aabir, getting to his feet. 'Your salary shall be doubled.'

'Aabir!' exclaimed Mrs Mookerjee, infuriated.

Azim's thunder-face crinkled into the first smile Geeta had seen. Almost immediately she felt her troubles wash away.

Purohitmoshai was not offered any of the exceptional posto-bora.

Aabir resumed his seat and squeezed Kimaya's hand under the table. 'Bring out the *gurer payesh*, Azim. It's just the day for it.'

Because too many cooks invariably spoil the broth, here's to everyone who spoilt this one

Hindol Sengupta, for the blog that started it all, for encouraging Urvashi Suraiya to rediscover sketching. I remain indebted to weightofpaper.blogspot.in and for being invited to add to its quaint pieces.

Uruashi Suraiya, who was reluctant to sketch but did it anyway, with all the earnestness that has defined her since we were in school.

Priya Doraswamy, my agent, for unwavering faith and encouragement, for always sounding jolly even after the fourth draft or so.

Dharini and Sneha, who loved the manuscript and made edits super-smooth.

The immediate familia, whose mad idiosyncrasies were inspiring and who didn't know this was in the making, which explains its completion.

Marcs, who shredded the first draft of this manuscript.

Mala Bose of Strawberry Chiffon Pie, who read the first draft and did not shred it, though she should have.

Cowboy, for being the willing proof-reader on draft one.

Achala, Pie and Geroy for being earnest cheerleaders, though I might have preferred an actual pom-pom dance to texts and emoticons.

Hunter, for always being brutal enough to spill the truth, the whole truth and nothing but the truth, so help him God.

Bum, doppel, fan and critic, who demands an original novella for her birthday every year and never gets tired of reading the nonsense that I write. Here's to the imaginative scribbling that has its roots in the last row of XI, Humanities.